ELIJAH'S
Whim

SHARK'S EDGE: BOOK SEVEN

VICTORIA BLUE

ELIJAH'S
Whim

SHARK'S EDGE: BOOK SEVEN

VICTORIA BLUE

WATERHOUSE PRESS

For David—my partner, my love,
my very best friend—I will love you always.
I appreciate your support and steadfastness
through this amazing life we've built together,
the two humans we created and shaped,
the business we've grown and nurtured,
and all the things we still have to discover.
What a joy to know you'll be by my side
as they reveal themselves!

CHAPTER ONE

ELIJAH

Monday mornings never looked good on me. I had a hard time letting go of the weekend debauchery in favor of a button-down shirt and knotted tie, regardless of how well I wore the look.

I chuckled to myself while knocking on the thick oak door. Yeah, humility had never been a good look for me either. Not that I gave that one too many laps around the track.

But I already knew this particular Monday was going to be a doozy. My two best friends were on the other side of that heavy panel, and they were going to pounce on me the moment I walked through the damn door.

It wasn't completely their fault. Lately, egging them on was one of the highlights of my otherwise boring life. The more weighed down they became with life's trappings, the easier they were to antagonize. Especially Sebastian, with a newborn son, baby mama Abbigail, and constructing his dream-turned-reality skyscraper dubbed the Edge in downtown Los Angeles's Financial District. It was like taking candy from a baby with him. A two-hundred-ten-pound, nothing-but-muscle, and really bad-tempered baby—but a baby all the same.

"In!" the big guy called from behind his desk—or where

I pictured him to be sitting when he gave his usual call to enter his office. I'd been on the other side of the door enough times when the mighty Sebastian Shark bellowed for someone to come in, not being bothered to stand up and greet his visitor.

As predicted, when I breached the entrance, Bas was seated behind his three monitors, already typing angrily on the keyboard in front of him. At the same time, striding toward me with his usual wide grin in place, was our six-and-a-half-foot-tall friend, Grant Twombley. The man was newly engaged and looking more and more like himself with every day that got between him and the nightmare abduction he recently endured. He reached forward to initiate our brotherly handshake.

"Ahh, speak of the devil," Grant said good-naturedly.

"How's it going, man? I will take that comparison every day of the week. But do I want to know what the two of you were talking about?"

"Maybe." He chuckled and then shrugged. "Maybe not. But it can't be too hard to guess."

"That bathing suit Rio was wearing at the pool party?" I waggled my brows wolfishly, but it was all an act.

Grant growled in my direction, and it was comical because he knew how I felt about his woman. My buddy couldn't think the comment was meant to do anything more than get a rise out of him. Could he? I actually had a moment of regret for saying it—but just for a millisecond. That he took that bait defied all reason.

"Why do you insist on egging him on, Elijah?" Bas asked, pinching the bridge of his nose. "And so early . . ."

"I know, I know," I said, holding my hands up in surrender.

"It's just too easy sometimes."

Time for a subject change before I was having to supplicate before my morning caffeine boost.

"Coffee top off, anyone?" I offered, strolling over to the boss's setup on the far side of his luxurious office. Floor-to-ceiling windows lined one side of the suite and offered one of the best views of downtown Los Angeles money could buy. Three of the ten wealthiest people in the city were accounted for in this very room. My two best friends and I were well acquainted with the finer things money could buy. However, the life lesson that remained the most important thus far was knowing the things you couldn't buy no matter how much money you had. And the three of us could check that damn box too.

When I turned back to face the other men, I realized I had some expectations as to what might happen next. Usually, we would go over to the sitting area of Bas's accommodating office suite. Two or possibly all three of us would make small talk as we slowly strolled there. I would notice, as I always did, how perfectly the nap of the carpet rested in one direction more than the other. And I would chuckle internally—of course—when remembering the way I would tease Shark that Terryn, his now dead administrative assistant, came in before everyone else started their day and crawled around on her hands and knees combing the shag into submission.

Now my theory was blown to hell since the nut burger was taking a permanent dirt nap and the rug's pile never looked better. It could've been Sebastian himself. He'd never been one to turn an aloof cheek to an overflowing toilet or a photocopier that was out of paper.

Expectations or not, we made our way to our unofficial

spots on the black leather furniture. Grant leaned back as though he were about to stretch his incredibly long legs out and prop them on the flat surface of the coffee table.

"Don't do it, brother," I advised with pain in my voice. The anguished sound was predictive emotion based on events of the past. No one wanted to sit through another one of the almighty Shark's lectures. Especially on the finer points of respecting someone else's property. The man was quick to forget we all grew up together. Like it or not, we'd watched each other go through every stage of every habit we'd ever had. Good, bad, and ugly.

Now, as we sat in the posh office, I marveled that we made it through to the other side of adolescence. We were boys, always living life in the fast lane and being too foolish to stop and analyze the danger involved in our antics. Because, at the same time, we were also smarter than anyone around us, as all young men are. We were sure we had it all figured out.

Even if someone had dared to tell us our plans were dumb or had holes, we never listened anyway. Frankly, we had nothing to lose. Each of us had a different reason why, but we were all robbed of that experience with our own parents—but at its core, we had that common bond.

We were young, reckless, and parentless. No one wanted us.

But we had each other, and that became everything.

"I'm just going to dig right in here, Banks," Grant warned.

"I expect no less," I said and then lifted my coffee mug to my lips and tried to hide my grin behind the thing.

But then the realization hit me. If we were going to get serious—right here and now—this place needed to be swept. To Bas, I asked, "When's the last time you had a proper cleaning crew in here?"

"Nice try, asshole," Grant responded. "You're not changing the subject that easily because you don't want to be in the spotlight for a change."

I already knew his head was so far up in Rio Gibson's beaver he would never catch the double meaning of what I was asking Sebastian. Hell, with the current state of Grant's love-addled mind, we'd likely have to carry him if we needed him to move quickly.

With efficiency, I strode to Bas's desk and snatched the pen and paper he held out for me. I scrolled a quick message on the paper and held it up for my tall friend to see. He nodded once while reading and then met my gaze. Together, we redirected our attention to Sebastian to find he was already on the move from behind his desk. He motioned for us to follow him out into the hall, and like the good little pups we were, we did just that.

There were so many times I felt frustrated with the follower role I was forced into when hanging out with Bas instead of assuming the leader role I was more suited to fill. On the rare occasions we topped a woman together, the power struggle between Bas and me was more exciting than the usual ho-hum between the woman and me. For that exact reason, I preferred sharing with Grant much more. Those confusing feelings never entered the dynamic, and I'd really rather keep it that way.

Once we were out in the hall, we all felt better about talking freely. After the last incident at Abstract Catering's prep kitchen, it seemed impossible to be too careful.

We followed Bas into the elevator, and he waved his building identification in front of the control panel. After punching in a series of numbers, the elevator ascended.

"We're going up?" Grant asked. "I thought we were on the top floor?"

"The roof," Bas said. His version of an explanation. "No one else has the code besides maintenance." Then, as an afterthought, he tacked on, "And first responders, of course."

"Of course," Grant and I mocked in harmony, using the same nonchalant tone Bas had used.

Surprisingly, there was a weathered aluminum patio set situated on the tar-papered roof about half the distance between the elevator shaft and the far ledge. There was even an old sun-bleached umbrella speared through a hole in the middle of the square table. Somehow the thing still provided a decent amount of shade, despite its dilapidated condition. Four chairs were neatly arranged around the table, and the whole scene looked as though a secret meeting of LA's Illuminati took place here on the first Tuesday of every month.

"At the risk of sounding cliché"—I paused midstride and waited for my two friends to stop and turn back toward me before delivering the punch line—"do you come here often?" I asked, unable to hold back the crooked grin that swept across my features.

"Very funny," answered Bas. "For the record, I come up here on the days I need to clear my head or just need to be alone."

Grant and I seemed to clue in on a shift in our best friend's body language or magnetic resonance, or—or hell only knows what it was that made us both pause and look at the man at the exact same time and then sneak a quick glance to one another. But Bas was drowning emotionally and had no idea how to save himself. It was safe to say these were waters Sebastian

Shark was not comfortable swimming in.

"Again, not to sound cliché, my brother, but you look like a fish out of water right now," I said. I thought we were coming up here to talk about new intel on the pirate situation, but Bas looked as green as a seasick tourist.

Grant threw his head back while belting out his infectious laughter, but Sebastian stood as stoically as before.

Grant looked from me to Bas and then threw his hands up in frustration. "Come on! You know that was funny. He said it intentionally to be funny. Why are you so uptight, dude?"

Humans were simple and entertaining creatures. I'd taken a deep interest in people watching at a very young age, and noticing the nuances of human behavior helped me to be an excellent con man when we were street urchins, and then it helped me be an outstanding businessman now that we were adults. The skill was invaluable with women, and it even helped with navigating through relationships with friends.

Like right now.

While Bas and Grant were preoccupied with their miniature spat, I casually motioned us toward the table and chairs. We each pulled out and brushed off a chair to sit on.

"Okay, Shark," I said to lead off our relocated meeting, "tell us what's going on. You know we always have your back."

Grant nodded and added, "But you have to loop us in."

"What makes the two of you so sure there is something going on with me?"

"I think I'd classify it as an atmospheric disturbance. How about you, Banks?" Grant asked, looking my way.

"That's not bad," I said while nodding. "Yeah, not bad at all."

"So out with it. Tell us what's going on," Grant issued while considering resting his arms in front of him on the table but immediately rethinking it when he saw how dirty the furniture was.

Bas heaved out a sigh and shifted his big frame in the rickety chair. The thing gave a protesting groan under his weight, and we all held our breaths, thinking his ass was about to hit the deck if a leg gave out. Finally, though, he said, "I think I'm fucking up my son. Already."

"Sebastian. Come on, man. Why would you say that?" Grant asked. He beat me to the question only by a fraction of a second.

Our normally take-charge friend looked like he was about to crumble though, so I knew admitting that fear took a lot out of him. The time for ribbing and horsing around had passed, because he needed his brother-close best friends more than anything in the moment.

"Bas. What is this about? Did something happen? Did Abbi say something to you that made you feel this way?" Then a thought hit me, and I sucked in a breath, ready to launch into a tirade once he confirmed my guess. "Or was it Dori? She seems a little too comfortable around you all for hired help, if you ask me."

Sebastian put up his hand to stop me from wandering down the path of distrust any further. At least out loud. I still couldn't help the weird twitch of suspicion I got every time that woman was in the room. If I ever found a free second in my day, digging into her background was on the top of my to-do list.

"No, no. Settle down, both of you. Damn, the pair of you are like pit bulls. What's with the protective shit?" Bas scowled as he looked from Grant to me and then back again.

"We care about you." Grant reached out to comfort Sebastian but quickly pulled back his hand. "I know, I know." He put his flat palm up in surrender.

Christ, Bas was in a mood today. Grant was simply going to touch his shoulder in reassurance, and he almost bit the thing off. Luckily Grant was particularly gregarious at the moment. Shit, who was I trying to kid? He had been this happy every moment since things were on track between him and Rio again. He was just better at morphing with our buddy's mood swings. That wasn't to say, however, that I wasn't on the receiving end of a few eye rolls and pleading glances conveying *Do something, man!*

"Sebastian, it's not unheard of for friends to feel defensive when they think someone may have"—I rolled my eyes heavenward, searching for the right terminology—"misguided intentions toward one of their own. Understand?"

"Yes, of course I do," he snapped. "You don't have to be an asshole and speak to me like I'm five."

"Well, sometimes I do. Especially when it comes to interpersonal relationships. But that's okay, because I love you, man, and I'm here to guide you through the scary world of feelings."

Saying that made my buddy cringe back from me like a vampire seeing sunlight, and I chuckled because I knew it would have that exact effect on him. At least he wasn't wallowing anymore.

"Now tell us what this is about. I'm sure you aren't fucking up your infant," I urged.

Bas took a steadying breath, seeming to come to a decision by the way he finally let his shoulders relax with his exhalation. "Well, I'm doing something wrong, and I can't figure out what it is. I read so many books while Abbi was pregnant. Seriously, it had to be at least ten." He leaned back in the creaky chair in frustration, and the whole thing complained that time, not just the legs. But Bas was on a roll. "Now that he's here, nothing is going as planned. He just doesn't like me. I think it's that simple." He looked from Grant to me for some sort of input, but before either of us could come up with something to lure him in off the ledge he had himself out on, he continued.

"Abbi holds him"—he shrugged—"he's totally fine. Happy, content, calm. But the minute I pick him up or she hands him to me, he cries. Nothing I do calms him down." He thrust both hands back through his perfectly styled hair in frustration before continuing. "So I've been studying what she does with him on the security cameras, you know, to get tips on how to be better at this whole parent thing. But I swear! I'm doing the exact same things she is!"

By the end of his speech, he was shouting. The poor man had himself so worked up over this, he was yelling about it. I didn't want to be insensitive and chuckle, but when I looked over to Grant—Bas's head now cradled in his palms—I saw he was beet red from holding in the same reaction.

Once Grant and I made eye contact, there was no going back. The dam burst, and we broke into a fit of raucous laughter.

"You know what?" Bas shouted, standing so abruptly that old chair finally gave in. But instead of rocking back like physics would've dictated, the decrepit seat crumpled in on itself to make an awkward and sad pile of metal and PVC right behind Sebastian's feet.

"You two are assholes," Bas continued. "You conned me into opening up to you, and when I finally did, you fucking laugh at me. You won't be laughing when you're in this situation." He stabbed his thick index finger to the top of the table, and the whole thing yawed to the left. We all lurched back after seeing what just happened to the chair, but Bas was on a roll, so he barely skipped a beat. He simply pointed his meaty finger in Grant's face instead.

"You'll see!" he ended with a shout, his broad chest pumping in and out with each breath.

"Calm down, Bas," I said, trying to be the diplomat. "We're not laughing at you. It's the situation that's a little funny. And I can't even say 'look at it from our perspective,' because you're too wound up to do that, too."

"He's probably sensing your tension," Grant said calmly, not remotely ruffled from Bas's outburst inches from his face.

"What?" Bas stopped his pacing and waited for Twombley to explain.

Grant shrugged. "I don't know. Isn't that a thing? Babies and animals can tell when you are scared or nervous or whatever. They can feel it in your aura or some shit."

"In my aura?" Sebastian looked at me for a long beat and then swung his head back to look directly at Grant again, then repeated, "In my *aura*? Are you fucking for real, man?"

"I don't know!" Grant threw his hands up in frustration then too. "Do you see a baby here with me? No! And that's precisely why. I don't know dick about them. But I sure as hell know how to *not* have one, though. Wear a damn condom, man!"

"Even I know it's a little late for that. And I think we can all agree I'm the furthest from ready to start a family," I said, trying to get these two to cool down. But when they both looked at me with the same expression on their faces, I felt like the one who was going to need a cool down.

"What?" I barked when they both just stared at me like I sprouted a second head.

"Dude," Grant said as though that were a chapter's worth of words of explanation.

"What?" I repeated, getting a little pissed, which I worked daily at not doing.

"Banks, come on. This is us," Bas said, gesturing a jerky triangle between the three of us. "We were there, remember?"

Goddammit. Why did it always come back to this? To her? I could run, but I couldn't hide. And even when I did forget about Ms. Hensley Pritchett and the upheaval she caused in my very carefully orchestrated existence, someone else was right there to remind me. But why did it have to be one of these two? It felt like a betrayal of the worst kind.

When I stared at the ground too long, Grant approached cautiously. No joke—cautiously.

"Elijah, look, we didn't mean anything by any of that. It was insensi—"

But I cut off his explanation. An explanation I wasn't interested in hearing or having to comment on afterward. "Just stop. I'm not your woman. You don't have to tiptoe around me in fear of my reaction to something you said that may have been out of line. The wildest I get with fire is in my fireplace, man."

When I finally looked up, I expected to find fury in his blue stare, and I was ready. I welcomed it—hoped for it, as a matter of fact. Instead, I was almost knocked to the ground by the pain I saw there. Because it was pain I caused, and I did it because I was a coward. I was no better than a playground bully.

But instead of fists, I used my words because I didn't want to face my own emotional scars. I lashed out at my dearest friend—my brother—all because he was trying to help me. These two men were better friends than I deserved. I let my head drop forward again until my chin hit my chest. Even when Grant began speaking, it took a few words before I leveled my gaze to his.

"That was uncalled for, and you know it," Grant said in a quiet, eerily calm voice. "Maybe lashing out is how you guard yourself from dealing with the past, Elijah, but I hope you don't lose people who truly care about you before you pull your head out of your ass."

With the same peaceful composure, he put his hands in the pockets of his slacks, turned, and walked toward the elevator. He never looked back before getting in the waiting car and presumably heading toward his office to finish his workday.

"Oh my God, I'm an asshole. Seriously. What's wrong with me? How do I let this woman still get to me like this? That man is one of the best things in my fucked-up life, and I just spoke to him like trash." I felt that awful feeling I usually did when all things Hensley were dragged up. That potentially panic-inducing sensation that started deep in my stomach and eventually—no matter what tricks I employed—managed to cut off my air supply completely.

But Bas was there to intercept the emotional deluge before it crested.

"Look, man..." He paused for a few beats longer than I would've liked. I ended up having to meet his agonized gaze too. "I think we all have a lot of balls in the air right now with personal shit. Then you add in this other bullshit." He sliced his hands back and forth aggressively, at once redirecting my concern solely on him.

"I'm so sorry, Sebastian."

"Why the hell are you apologizing to me?" he growled.

"Because," I answered, as if it were as obvious as the chances of it being another sunny day in SoCal. Once the June gloom burned off, at least.

"Because this conversation started with you looking for advice on how to handle your fatherly frustrations, and it turned into another episode of the Hensley halftime show." I scrubbed my hand down my face and then yelled, "Fuck me! How I'd wish that woman would just get out of my head! My history!" Finally, having gotten that out of my system, I sucked in a cleansing breath through my nose, during which time, thank all things that were holy, Sebastian said nothing.

Then I quietly muttered, "My heart."

With equally calm patience, my buddy asked, "Is she really still there? Your heart, I mean? How can that be? I just don't get it. After all the drama and all the anguish. How do you still have room inside you for that poisonous bitch?"

I just shook my head. I knew why Bas and Grant felt the way they did. And I loved them for every bit of it. Their loyalty was more than I could ever dream of deserving from another person, let alone two. But in my darkest hours, I was ashamed to accept that kind of allegiance from anyone. Because it was passion I didn't earn.

Grant and Sebastian didn't know the whole story and likely never would. They didn't know the whole truth behind my history with Hensley Pritchett and why the gash she cut into my heart—and, frankly, my entire world—ran so deep. After her betrayal, I never trusted anyone with my truth, not even them. If my two best friends knew that little tidbit, they would probably be cut to the bone with hurt and anger. Because we always had each other's backs, and our friendship had always had a resounding foundation of family deep trust. If the three of us had nothing else, we always had each other.

But I had let a woman in closer than them, and I always feared they would consider this a sort of unfaithfulness to them. I wasn't bullshitting when I told them they were the only people in this entire world I cared about and probably ever would. So how did I explain letting her in on the darkest parts of my life when not even they knew about those times? I knew the reasons why I never weighed them down with my full history, but trying to explain that kind of shit to two of the most complicated men who ever existed outside myself? Yeah, well, we were a therapist's dream for sure.

Fuck me.

The list of reasons to loathe myself grew by the day, so I stuffed it all down and tried not to think about any of it. Until someone brought up that woman's name, and then my house of cards came tumbling down around me and I'd lash out like I just had.

They had no idea the danger the woman still was to every breath of air I breathed as a free man and why she would continue to be as long as I lived. I'd made the mistake of baring myself to her in the afterglow of sex—sex I foolishly mistook for love. And then she walked out on me. After that, I swore I'd never make the same mistake again. I'd never let another woman get close to my heart, to my very soul, like she had. No woman would ever have this kind of power over me again.

No one would.

CHAPTER TWO

HANNAH

"Seriously?" While I issued the question into the still air that filled the modern kitchen, my ire ensured my tone was grittier. The single word bounced off a few flat surfaces before making a lonely lap around the cavernous room and landing back in my ears, sounding bitter and potentially destructive.

I quickly gulped down the tea I'd been nursing just so I'd have something to busy my hands with when Elijah strolled in the door from work.

Strolled was definitely the right verb here. Ambled would have also worked.

"Perfect," I mumbled into my mug before the liquid touched my lips again. I took a gulp now that it was much cooler and finished my thought. "Now I'm talking to myself, too. Just perfect."

What the hell had I gotten myself into? I shook my head and thought of the events of the past few days. My intuition was one of my best qualities, or so I'd thought. This Elijah Banks fellow seemed like a nice enough man. Sure, he was arrogant, irritating, and a bit condescending when certain topics were brought up, but overall, he seemed like a genuinely good man. He cared deeply for his friends and was honest and loyal to those inside his closest circle.

With the afternoon sun dropping below the bottom edge of the roman shades, a blinding beam of beautiful orange sunlight came through every westerly window in the kitchen and family room. I was a little surprised my uptight host didn't have the window coverings on some sort of timer so the exact second one ray of natural light hit his pristine home it was blocked, the spot immediately sterilized, and then every step taken to reverse the damage. Visualizing the chain of events made a laugh bubble up and spurt out like boiling water from an overfilled tea pot.

I folded my forearms over each other and buried my face inside the bunker I'd created there. My sisters and I used to talk about the best place to hide if we could make our bodies any size. A trusted friend's pocket was always my favorite option until my sister, Shep, pointed out all the flaws in my plan.

She was always the dream killer. Still to this day, if there was a way to take the wind out of someone's sail, Sheppard Farsey would find it. When I'd told her once she was too jaded for someone so young, she even had a contrary response to that.

"I'm not jaded, Hannah. I'm realistic," she had said. "There's a difference."

"Shep, you haven't seen enough of the world yet to be *realistic*. I just don't know what you're basing all your *realism* on." I'd said it with focused attention on that particular word and truly hoped she would have an answer this time. But she never did, and we'd move on to the next topic we never agreed on, and so it would go.

Funny how people took things for granted when they were right under their noses. Then when they didn't have those same things anymore, they missed them like crazy.

I was having a grade-A pity party for myself, and it all felt so foreign. Like I was trying on someone else's favorite pair of jeans. They neither fit nor were a style I liked, but I kept trying to make them work, but instead, the whole exercise was doing the exact opposite. Instead of comforting me, I felt even more out of sorts. When I tried to relieve some of the expectations and high standards I imposed on myself, my skin felt too tight—almost itchy to the point of burning. Perfection was my comfort zone, and I'd been trying to make peace with it my entire life.

I rolled my neck from side to side to alleviate some of the energy bottled up in the muscles corded between my shoulder blades, but it was no use. Once the ball of tension nested there, I had a hard time working it out. It was unusual to get this tense this late in the day. Normally my after-work routine was for myself. Over the past week, however, nothing was falling into the category of normal.

Just as I finished that realization, the biggest factor of change entered the room. The mighty, mouthwatering Elijah Banks himself.

He'd given me a laundry list of rules he wanted me to follow inside and outside this ridiculously large and perfectly kept castle. For the most part, these were things that would make us look like a couple. Some of the things were out in left field, but Elijah insisted they were perfectly normal in a Dominant/submissive relationship. He was well known in that community, so if someone saw him with a woman who was not behaving a certain way, it would attract attention for that point alone. When I tried to argue it was unnecessary behind closed doors, of course he disagreed, saying I needed the training to stay in proper form.

Jesus Christ, whatever that meant.

There was sure to be a lecture in my near future because I was supposed to greet him at the door like a good little housewife. But I couldn't bring myself to care about that. Never mind that I also worked all day and I was tired and my body was aching—two things I didn't normally deal with from my day at Abstract. Even though a professional kitchen was the epitome of stressful, I loved the fast-paced environment and thrived there. It was my comfort zone—my happy place.

So maybe killing this man with kindness would work better than ignoring him the way I tried yesterday. Yeah, let's just say I found out very quickly that he didn't care for that approach. Somebody must've been a spoiled brat while growing up and was used to all the attention and getting his way immediately. Poor guy would've been reduced to emotional roadkill if he grew up in a household like mine.

When a Farsey child needed our parents' attention, she basically had to take a number like a deli counter customer and wait patiently until it was announced overhead. Only an actively bleeding wound could gain you head-of-line privileges. If the blood was already clotted or dried? Sorry, sister! You were doomed to the waiting game like everyone else.

"Good evening, Mr. Banks. I hope your day was excellent. I was just about to retire for the evening, so I'm glad I got to see you before I did. I'll see you tomorrow." I plastered on my megawatt competitive cheer smile and stood from where I had been sitting at the island.

But Elijah moved like a panther. Quickly and silently, he was right beside me, blocking me in.

"Excuse me, Elijah." I gasped while fluttering my hand to my throat. "I just said I'm turning in for the night."

"Why are you pushing me like this? Every day this week, I've come home and you've disobeyed me in one way or another." He took a step closer.

All I could do was lean back. My feet were trapped in place by the heavy stool on one side and Elijah's feet on the other.

As if he weren't invading my personal space with his entire body, he continued with the lecture. "I've let it go without punishing you, but I see leniency was a mistake. Maybe you crave punishment?" he answered with smug assuredness.

"Punishment? Be serious, man. What era do you live in?" Well, so much for my cheerful demeanor. This guy brought out the worst of my temper. "And back up. You're invading my personal space, and I don't appreciate it."

He chuckled at my comment. Actually laughed. I would've kneed him in the balls if I weren't confined by the damn counter stool and his incredibly enticing body.

Fine. So I'd noticed his body. But in my defense, he swam laps every morning in one of those bike-shorts-style bathing suits, and holy Christ—his body.

"How old are you, gorgeous?"

"My name is Hannah."

"Stop acting so prim. It's a compliment. And answer the question."

"Then … thank you," I said very quietly while looking past him to zero in on the base molding across the room. "If you'll excuse me, Mr. Banks, I'm heading to my room for a long bath and then bed. That clawfoot masterpiece in my bathroom has been taunting me since I got here."

There. I was polite. I gushed over his gigantic, albeit sterile, house and even accounted for my personal time. Not that it was any of his business. I should be home free.

"Let me get you set up. What kind of host would I be if I didn't?"

"Don't be ridiculous. It's a bath. I'm sure I can manage. Plus, you just got home. I'm sure you want dinner, and you normally have a guest over in the evening. Don't let me interrupt your routine," I offered, backing out of the kitchen.

And yes, fine. I'd also taken notice of the revolving door leading to and from his bedroom. Whatever. He didn't owe me an explanation.

The man stared at me for a few seconds too long, and I turned on my heel so fast, I felt my loose hair fan out behind me like a Flamenco dancer's skirts. I scurried off toward my room at the opposite end of the house.

The suite had a sitting room, bathroom, and bedroom. Like the rest of the house, these rooms were exquisitely decorated with understated elegance. Next time I was feeling like shooting the breeze with my captor—pardon me—host, I'd have to ask him who his interior designer was. Elijah was an asshole on many levels, but he had incredible taste when it came to architecture, fashion, and art. If it pleased the senses, he had it on lock.

Since I was dipping my toe in the pool of fairness, I had to admit he wasn't holding me here at his home against my will, but this infuriating man could make me uncomfortable with the twitch of a single eyebrow. He could test my patience with his knack for riddling me with too many questions about my process for any number of things, too.

My heart felt like it was hammering in my chest by the time I reached my room, and I slammed the door shut a bit harder than necessary.

I sighed while looking at my reflection in the mirrors

around the vanity, where I sat to brush through my hair before getting in the tub. The enormous white clawfoot tub was filling with steaming-hot water from plumbing that came up out of the floor and disappeared into the ceiling overhead. The polished chrome pipes were exposed so one could visually follow the bends and curves down toward the floor. Another separate pipe came up out of the floor and proudly shot straight up and bowed over the tub basin like a faithful man praying. On the end was a mushroom-capped spigot head where the water dispersed however the bather liked it.

The rooms I was set up in were more like a spa than someone's home. Elijah went all out with everything he took on, and my mind wandered down a dangerous path. There was no way I had what it would take to keep a man like him satisfied, but he would give me some fun fantasy material while I stayed here. I would definitely be grilling Rio the next time I was sure it was safe to do so.

No.

I stared up at the plaster ceiling after pulling my T-shirt over my head.

No, no, no.

I repeated the monosyllabic word in my head over and over and let my arms flop down to my sides. By unclasping my grip on the cotton fabric, my sweaty T-shirt plopped to the floor. It seemed like my good mood was headed in the same direction.

Elijah and I had agreed it would never be safe to talk to anyone else about our plan. We had to stick to the script one hundred percent, or it wouldn't work. If someone was watching Abstract or me . . . or both—like he suspected they were—it was only a matter of time before they launched a new attack. Then

I would be in even bigger danger than I was before. Before, I was just a random girl in the wrong place at the wrong time. Now, I was an identified threat. A known problem.

A new target.

These were the things I reminded myself of when I got homesick, too. I needed to keep my parents and sisters at arm's length to keep them out of harm's way. It was really just that simple.

After disrobing completely, I lifted one leg over the side of the tub and tested the water with my toe before plunging my entire foot in. Cooking all these years had not toughened me up like so many people—namely, my sisters—thought it would. I was still a prima donna where extreme anything was concerned. Careful and comfortable was right where I liked to be. Unless I was ballooning. Then I didn't have a single care in the world.

The bubble bath I found beneath the sink was heavenly. The suds were like velvet on my skin, and the smell was divine. It was sensual and inviting, yet not overpowering or cloying. I didn't inspect the bottle, but my guess was that it was amber or sandalwood. Vetiver was definitely involved in the bathroom somewhere, but I wasn't sure if it was a candle or fabric softener used on the towels. Whatever the combination, it was complete perfection. I could have easily fallen asleep. With my eyes closed and my head resting back on the turned lip of the tub, I was in my own little cocoon of tranquility.

"I have never wanted to be soap suds so badly in my life," I thought I heard a deep—and, might I add, sexy as sin—voice say.

I popped one eye open to look around the room, about eighty percent sure I'd lost my mind and was hearing voices now, too. But no, my imagination was not toying with me. Elijah Banks, my current landlord, was kneeling there, bent arms on the tub, chin in the cradle of his palm, staring down at me with deep consideration.

And let me just say Mr. Furley he was not. But shit—he could come knock on my door. My first impulse was to leap up and grab for my towel, but I quickly remembered I never pulled one off the towel bar in the first place. That action plan would've had me standing in front of the dude for way longer than I was comfortable. Right now, a half second would've been longer than I was comfortable.

Well...unless he kept looking at me exactly the way he was. But only then.

My second inclination was to yell and curse and shake my fist in his beautiful face and demand to know what gave him the nerve to think he could just barge in here like he owned the place and say—oh, wait...shit. He *did* own the place.

Well, there went that argument. By sliding a little deeper in the water, I made sure all my unmentionables were completely covered.

"Are you always this modest? You know it's just us in this entire house. Most of the time, anyway," Elijah said while keeping his stare riveted to mine. A lazy grin quirked up the one side of his mouth as he finished his comment.

Better to answer his question with another question, I figured. Rather than be in the hot seat, I'd put him there instead. I'd never met a guy who didn't love talking about himself. And one as pretty as Elijah? This guy probably couldn't stop once you pulled the string in the middle of his back.

"Are you?" I smiled sweetly while asking.

"We're not talking about me right now," he said in answer.

"No?" I tilted my head to the side. "We should be."

"We might be roommates for a long time, so I'd like to get to know you better. Plus, we're supposed to be pulling off a"—he leaned back to use both hands to make air quotes—"*relationship* here. Especially with the type we're going for. It's a unique bond built on complete trust. Yours and mine."

"Okay," I answered, but I didn't dare move a muscle in fear soap suds would shift and key places would no longer be covered.

"Okay? That's all you're going to give me?"

"Mr. Banks—"

"Elijah," he corrected instantly.

I sighed heavily. "Fine, Elijah. I don't want to have a conversation with you while I'm naked and you're dressed."

"Oh, got it, you want me naked too? I'd be more than happy." He stood up fast and whipped his shirt over his head, and suddenly I couldn't breathe. "To accommodate you. You are my guest, after all."

Literally, could not move air in or out of my lungs.

But when he yanked on the end of his belt to free the black leather from its other half, I found my voice. I had to stop him before he was out of his pants too.

"No. Stop."

"Why?" He looked up from the belt that, by some stroke of luck, was giving him mechanical trouble. "Fucking Burberry," he grumbled while messing with the belt again.

"That's what you get for straying from the double G's, dude." I gave him a quick wink when he looked up in surprise.

"What? A chef can't like nice things?"

"Of course she can. She should. I just haven't seen you out of those abysmal clown pants you wear along with that giant lab coat. How you don't catch fire cooking with all that extra fabric hanging off you, I'll never understand." He shook his head with a wide grin on his sinfully beautiful mouth.

"What's the smile about? It can't be over that joke. It wasn't even funny."

After narrowing his eyes in a look that I guessed was supposed to be menacing, he sobered and said, "I was thinking about the first time I saw Rio in her real clothes. I couldn't believe how small she was. I had only ever seen her in all that chef stuff."

He gave his head a little shake and totally surprised me with his next question. The subject shift was so incongruous.

"So, what do you think of Gucci's Fall and Winter line?"

Beneath the surface, I made gentle swirls with my hands to circulate the water. It was getting a little cool, but now that we were having a normal conversation, I didn't want it to end.

"What I've seen so far, I like. I didn't see much fashion week activity this year, but I try to keep up with a few bloggers and influencers who really seem to have their finger on the industry's pulse."

"Are you getting cold? Your water must be cooling off. I can leave you—"

"No—"

He studied my face with quiet consideration. The way he had his hands slung casually in his pockets was so arousing. Fine. Who was I kidding? Everything about this guy was arousing. His pockets standing alone in the corner by themselves would be arousing. Simply because they were his.

"I just mean—well, I don't know what I mean. I was enjoying talking with someone. It's lonely here for me. I'm used to a household with a handful of siblings and two parents.

It's near chaos at all times. Here, well—"

"It's not. I get it." He grabbed a fluffy towel off the towel bar by the shower enclosure and held it up for me to step into. "Come. Let's dry you off, then. We can talk more."

"Elijah."

"Hmmm?"

"Drying off isn't a team sport. I think I can manage."

"Is there a reason you don't want me to see your body? Are you covered in tattoos?" he asked while walking toward the foot of the tub.

"No, of course not. I don't have a single one, actually."

"I didn't think a good girl like you would." Casually, he reached into the water and pulled the rubber stopper out of the drain. "Now what will you do? Let me wrap you in this towel, or let the water drain away completely and go get your own towel?"

"Get out!" I shouted. He had to go and ruin things with his high-handedness. "You're such a jerk."

"Not a chance, beautiful. And if you'd let your damn guard down, you'd see I'm the furthest thing from a jerk. Come."

"I don't trust men like you. Come over here at least. I don't want to parade across the room. I can get my own towel at that point."

Well, at least I was still mostly covered in soap suds. So, on nervous legs, I stood and got out of the tub. Elijah steadied me so I wouldn't slip on the wet tile, and all I could think about was how clumsy I must have looked climbing over the high wall of the tub. He probably just had a better view of my vagina than my lady parts doctor got during my annual exam.

I buried my face in my palms and waited for the whole thing to just be over. Christ, I'd never been so embarrassed in my life. I'd bet his nightly visitors never felt this awkward. Why was he putting me through this?

With a victorious grin on his lips, he came close enough that I could smell his intoxicating scent, made even more potent by the humidity in the bathroom. His strong hands felt so capable as he swaddled me in the terry cloth. But that damn ache in my shoulders was right back where it started from the stress of having to bare myself to him.

This was ridiculous. *I* was being ridiculous. With one hand, I took the ends of the towel, and with the opposite, I kneaded the tense muscle in my shoulder. "Umm, thanks." I felt as awkward as I did on my parents' front doorstep junior year of high school when Connor Billings brought me home from my first date and moved in for a good-night kiss.

Thumbing over my sore shoulder, I said, "I think I'm just going to head to bed after all. I guess I'll see you tomorrow."

"Come." Elijah took my hand and towed me along behind him into the bedroom.

"I'm not your pet. Stop saying that to me." I scowled and tried to pull my hand free.

He turned to face me, and I swear on my cat, Molly, in heaven, with just the bedside lamp lit behind him, he looked like a damn angel. The man was that arrestingly handsome.

"Actually, *beautiful* is what you are. And I've not been doing a very good job taking care of you. That's the fifth time I've seen you rub your shoulder since I've been home, and it's unacceptable. Now, since we haven't gotten to know each other in all the best ways yet"—he playfully waggled his eyebrows—"I will let you decide if you want me to rub the knot out of your shoulder while wearing the towel or not."

Even though it would likely get me in trouble—and

that thought had me inwardly rolling my eyes—I couldn't stop the comment I made next. "What's wrong with what you have on?"

Faster than I could track, he reached forward and snatched the towel right off me.

"Without. Perfect. On the bed, beautiful. Get comfortable facedown while I get some supplies."

While he strode from the room after issuing his set of instructions, I snatched the throw off the foot of my bed and held it to my chest. Although what did it matter at this point? He'd already seen my whole package. Lock, stock, and barrel, as my father and his gun club buddies would say.

I guessed the upside was he didn't run screaming from the room. At the same time, this dude had had a female visitor every night since I'd been staying here. I couldn't be sure if it was the same female or not. It wasn't as though he brought them by my room first for my approval before having his way with them. Point being, he'd seen his share of tits and asses by now. What difference was one more set going to make?

"Ms. Farsey…" His low rumble startled me from my own musings, and I jumped when he said my name with such wicked promise. Warm breath fanned across the back of my neck as he spoke the rest of his question.

"Did you do well at Le Cordon Bleu?"

"When measured by wha-what?" I asked, having learned quickly not to assume anything where Elijah Banks was concerned. Was he talking about traditional letter grades?

"You don't follow directions very well for a woman as bright as you are. I can't make sense of that. Are you defying me personally or this arrangement you agreed to?"

I spun to look at him face-to-face. If I was going to deny

his accusation, I wanted to do it head on. "No. Neither. That's not it at all."

"On. The. Bed."

Lifting one knee to the mattress, I turned back to give one last feeble protest and was met with a delicious, dominant man instead.

"Now."

"All right, all right. Jeez Louise. You can be so bossy."

"Oh, you haven't seen bossy, baby. But you will. Give it time."

CHAPTER THREE

ELIJAH

Forever. It had literally been forever—maybe even forever and a day—since I'd been this intrigued and excited by a female. Right now, the stunning bombshell fidgeting on the bed in front of me was doing both of those things in spades.

Her innocence had a lot to do with her appeal, there was no doubt about that fact. That in itself was unusual, since I was a dirty, twisted guy when it came to my sexual preferences. Those adjectives and innocent girls like Hannah Farsey didn't usually play well together.

So, for starters, I was going to have to get her to trust me enough to open up to me. Even just a little, because right now, she sure as hell didn't at all. And she didn't even know a thing about me. Unless . . .

Rio.

It had to be. Where else would she be getting this bad taste in her mouth? By now, I usually had women tripping all over themselves, and they couldn't even understand why, let alone explain it to their girlfriends. But Rio Gibson and I had gotten off on the wrong foot. Maybe even the wrong *feet*—that was how awkward and strained our relationship was.

Hannah worked for Rio and Abbigail, Sebastian's fiancée. Although, since Abbi was still on maternity leave, she wasn't coming into the kitchen every day. No one was there to balance all the negativity Rio was likely putting into the atmosphere with regard to me.

Well, I'd put an end to that bullshit first thing tomorrow.

"How about we get to know each other a little better while I work my magic?" I asked while twisting her hair into a tight rope and clipping that on top of her head to keep it out of the way.

She laughed. *Fucking laughed.* I also couldn't tell you the last time a woman laughed at me, but this one was full of surprises, if nothing else. In the meantime, the crotch of my pants just kept getting tighter and tighter. Her alto voice was like a vise on my balls in the best way. But even when she laughed? Yeah, at this pace, I was going to split the seam of this pair by the end of night.

"And what, might I ask, is so funny about that question? Actually, hold that answer. Are you allergic to anything? I have oil here for your neck and shoulder, and I want to be sure you don't have allergies to anything."

"No, I don't. Well, bees, but I don't think that will be a problem. Thank you for asking first, though."

She buried her face in the crook of her arm and finally settled in so I could rub her shoulder, but now I was torn. She should've told me about the bee allergy before we went to Bas and Abbi's pool party but didn't.

I wanted to address the issue immediately, but because it had taken her so long to finally relax into the idea of me massaging her shoulder, I made a mental note—and underlined it twice—to have the bee allergy conversation as soon as the massage was done.

"God, where did you learn to do this? Tell me you're a

massage therapist in your spare time, and I'm going to move in with you permanently," Hannah mumbled.

"Feel good?" I pushed for additional kind words instead of addressing her comment. I didn't want to sound too eager and freak her out.

"Yes. My shoulder already feels better than it was," she purred.

"Anything else hurting? What about your feet? You're on them all day."

"Are you trying to earn sainthood this evening, Mr. Banks?" Hannah asked after turning her face to the side to look at me.

I quickly squatted down to be eye level with her so she wouldn't see the massive erection I had. The grin that won me favors with women near and far slid into place as effortlessly as signing my name. I stroked her mussed hair back from her forehead and was again transfixed by her natural beauty. For a few moments, I just drank her in. She studied me as long as I studied her. And the whole time, I couldn't stop stroking my fingers through her silky hair.

"This has to be natural," I finally said, my eyes darting around her crown at all the shades of gold, white, yellow, and even a strand or two of red.

"It is." Her voice was still in the lower range I was officially insane for. But when her shy smile was coupled with that throaty rasp, my brain and dick were short-circuiting at the same time. No blood supply plus excessive blood supply equaled grown man down. It was simple biology and math.

I finally unscrambled my motherboard long enough to realize that her mouth had been moving, which probably meant she had been saying something and would expect a response of some type. I had to stop thinking with my dick, or I was going to come off like every other asshole who wanted in her pants—and who I wanted to now murder—and figure out what she had been saying this whole time.

"Why did you say 'it has to be,' though? I'm curious what you based that on."

Oh, thank fuck. Still about the hair. Seriously. Only women could go on this long about their hair.

"Well, for one thing, it feels so silky. Most women I've known who have had bottle blond?" I waited for her to respond in some way, so when she did with a nod, I continued. "I guess it felt dry or maybe damaged? Like it would go up in flames if she got too close to a heat source, you know?"

"Elijah!" She punched my arm playfully, but shit, the girl had a good hook on her.

Rubbing my arm, I whined a bit more than necessary. "Owww. Take it easy, killer. Hey, maybe when I have your collar made, I could have spikes put on it, and it can say Bruiser. Or, no, better! Killer!"

The next three things happened in quick, measured intervals, but there was no way to misunderstand her body language. I'd pushed her too far with that comment, and even though I was joking, all traces of humor were gone now.

First, her playful smile dropped away completely and her lips formed a stern line. Her azure eyes were opened as wide as possible so she wouldn't miss a single detail of my impending screw-up.

And the final clue, and likely the most potent of them all, was the methodical clip to each word when she all but hissed, "You can't be serious."

No, but she sure as shit was. And suddenly playtime was

over and she was taking her ball and going home. Clearly, I caused the final foul, but I needed to find out what I did and how to fix it. Quick.

I scrambled to my feet, and then in one easy motion, like mounting a surfboard to paddle out past the break, I covered her body with mine. With my stomach to her back, I used all my weight to press her into the mattress. There was no way this woman was going to throw me out of a room in my own house. And even though a small handful of women would disagree, I was a gentleman. *Fine.* A good, well-mannered man at the very least. So if that happened, I would do what she asked.

What I didn't tolerate, however, were women who stomped around like little brats. In my house, little brats got big spankings, and they usually didn't like them. Rarely did reality live up to fantasy, and a spanking for discipline was no different.

Now, a spanking for pleasure? That was a whole different story. The thought of spanking Ms. Farsey's perfectly peachy ass made me groan out loud. Forgetting I was still on top of her, I dropped my head to muffle the sound and ended up nuzzling my face right into her silky mane.

Good Christ. Out of the frying pan and into the fire.

I didn't want to let her go without addressing the topic at hand, but I had to roll off her immediately. I felt the undeniable stirring low in my balls, and I knew what followed close on the heels of that sensation. She would not miss the erection that I was about to regain if I didn't move.

With as much nimbleness as possible, I moved from atop her delectable body to the center of the bed. I didn't want her to feel trapped, and if I lay on the outside, she wouldn't have been able to get off the bed if she chose to do so.

Hannah looked confused and bewildered and still quite pissed off when our gazes met. How had I not noticed the lively way her blue eyes expressed so much emotion before?

"What?" she nearly growled, and damn if it didn't turn me on more.

"You're stunning," I answered with an honesty I hadn't tapped into in a very long time.

"And you're so full of shit your eyes should be brown instead of this icy magic you have going on here."

I couldn't help the grin that sneaked out after a comment like that. How was I even expected to keep it held in?

"I'm sorry I offended you earlier. It was not my intention, and I hope you'll forgive me." She went to speak, but I pressed a few fingers over her lips. I had one more thing I wanted to say before she tore into me again. "When you're ready to listen, I'd like the chance to explain what I was talking about. When you're ready, though." I moved my fingers from her plush mouth and was immediately sorry to not have that connection with her. It felt so damn good to be touching her anywhere—everywhere—I could be.

After inhaling a long breath, she let her eyes fall closed—and stayed that way for long moments. Of course, I didn't mind. Not one bit, because I studied her intensely while she relaxed. I wanted to pepper her with questions, but more than my own selfish desires, I wanted her to relax and have some peace. Her body had been so tense when I'd gotten home from work. I knew much of that was my fault. I wasn't always easy to be around. Of course, compared to, say, Bas, I was Mary fucking Poppins, but the more I got to know her, I didn't think I could let Hannah near someone like Bas.

"You have no idea how badly I want to touch you right

now," I said so quietly, I wondered if she heard me. It was possible it was very strong desire and not actually spoken words. If that were the case, I'd be safe from making an ass out of myself if I were rejected.

Rejected. There was a word that was bitter on the tongue and left an aftertaste similar to vomit for a guy with an ego the size of mine. It wasn't a concept I spent too much time on. Like stepping stones in a creek—you hopped quickly on to the next thing and never got too comfortable in that one place for very long.

"Where?"

That brought my attention back to the stunner right in front of me.

"Wha-What?" Shit. Was I on my first date?

Damn it, man, pull yourself together.

"Sorry. I was lost in a bit of a fantasy," I admitted honestly.

"Is that right?" She stole my half grin then, and damn if it didn't look good on her. "Are you going to share?"

"Oh, hell no." I chuckled lightly.

"That doesn't seem fair. So now you have to answer my first question. And don't be cheesy, either."

"Cheesy? *Moi?*"

"Oh, don't even. I doubt that innocent bit works on anyone, Elijah Banks. Now, before you kill the mood completely here…"

"Okay. Okay." I was a desperate man. "Let's recreate the scene." I wiggled from the shoulders down—the best I could while lying in a bed. Whatever the gesture looked like, it made Hannah laugh again, and I swear this woman's laugh was a bigger aphrodisiac than all the oysters in the Gulf of Mexico.

Once her eyes were closed, I said very quietly, "You have

no idea how badly I want to touch you right now." The full smile that split my face couldn't be helped. It was so damn good to be silly with Hannah and just feel alive with this captivatingly beautiful woman.

"Where?" she breathed.

This time I was ready with my answer. "Your ears."

She popped one eye open in the cutest, most curious way. "Seriously?"

"Trust me," I responded, keeping my voice seductive, even though hers had gone right into that snarky tone it did when she said that damn word. I already knew what was going to be the first item on her banishment list when we really got into our roles of this new relationship. That godforsaken word.

"Isn't it pretty obvious that I do?"

"That you do what, beautiful?"

"Trust you. It's probably the dumbest thing I've done to date, but for some reason, I do, Elijah. I trust you."

"I won't let you down, Hannah. Definitely not here in this bed. Ever. And I will do my very best to not let you down elsewhere, either," I promised the new obsession in my life while staring right at her.

"Now close your eyes. Let me make you feel good."

Of course, she had to ask more questions first. "Is this a good spot? Can you reach—my ears?" She rolled her eyes on the last words, and I bit into my cheek with the effort it took to hold back a reprimand.

"Now that you mention it, I'd like to sit up a little and have you put your head on my thigh. Would you be okay with that? Comfortable, I mean?"

"Yes. Thank you for asking," Hannah answered with a sweet shyness I'd only seen a bit of this evening. I'd seen embarrassed and angry but just a little shyness. And damn if every single emotion on this woman wasn't alluring.

"Of course. I never want you to do something you don't want to do. In my house, you always have the option of saying no. Always," I reassured her while she rearranged herself on my lap. She had no idea the pleasure she was in for, and like so many other things, I knew awakening her body as well as her mind and spirit was going to give me nearly as much pleasure as it was going to give her.

Nearly.

"Would it be easier for you if I put my hair up? Out of the way?"

"Definitely, but I don't want you to have to get up again. We can make do."

"I have something on the nightstand, if you wouldn't mind handing me the ponytail holder?" she asked sweetly and then followed her request with that sexy, husky laugh, and I had to close my eyes and beg my dick not to go rogue on me.

Not now, man.

"Why are you laughing? Do I want to know?" I asked, giving her a playfully menacing glare.

"I was thinking a big, bad, dominant man like you couldn't possibly know what a ponytail holder is. I don't know"—she shrugged—"for some reason, it's funny to me. I'm just being goofy. Without my sisters around, I have all this bottled-up silliness, seriousness, sadness, and even happiness. I'm used to having six other people to share it with." She gave another quick shrug. If I hadn't been watching her so intently, I would have missed it.

"Sit up for a second, beautiful," I said, kneeling on the bed behind her, ponytail holder held between my teeth.

I promised myself while I worked her long, glorious hair into a loose braid down the center of her back that I would get this woman back to her family as soon as possible. Even though I wanted to be a selfish bastard and keep her for myself, I'd rather have her happy and come to me by her own choice than for her to be here and miserable.

I would have to keep reminding myself of that vow over the next few weeks. Because given the way my dusty, cobweb-covered heart was already excitedly tumbling around inside my chest, I couldn't imagine what was going to be happening inside there in a month or two.

For now, though, I'd set that aside and enjoy the breathtaking blonde wiggling her way to comfort and using my thigh as her pillow. Thank fucking God my dick was resting down the other side at the moment or I was going to have to call this whole thing off. That or explain the unique anatomy I had been dealing with since puberty.

I never called it a problem, though, because really, what man in his right mind would call an abnormally large penis a problem? Sure, there were some things that were inconvenient about having a really big dick. But over time, I'd learned a lot of workarounds. The other times? Well, there wasn't much I could do. This was my body, and I did the best I could with it. From what I understood, my best was pretty fucking amazing.

The oil I used earlier on her shoulders was still on the night table, so I used a very small amount on my fingertips and traced the shell of Hannah's ears. Working in continuous motion from the inside ridge outward, I followed the natural curve of her cartilage with my slick fingers until I came down low to the slightly thicker pad of her earlobe.

When she was relaxed and pliant, I joined longer strokes

down to rub her sore shoulder again and after a few laps around from her ear, down her neck and to her shoulder, she was purring—and then quietly moaning.

"Elijah . . ." Hannah said my name with an enticing sexual lilt. I wasn't sure if it was involuntary, but I sure as hell planned to encourage it.

"You can moan all you want, beautiful. We're the only ones here, and it's so hot when you do that. Your voice alone . . ." I inhaled harshly through my nose, and I sounded like a bull getting ready to charge its target. "But the sounds coming from you when you're aroused? Jesus fuck, woman, I may need a minute or two alone in the bathroom."

"I thought you just said we're the only ones here," she replied without opening her eyes.

"That's right." My answer was more out of curiosity as to where she was going with her comment while I continued to stimulate her through one of my personal favorite and most unexpected massage techniques.

"Then why go in the bathroom? I won't stop you from doing what you need to do. It's your house, after all." Keeping her eyes closed, she gave that lazy grin I saw earlier, and I really wondered if she'd stolen my trick or if she'd always done it. Whatever the case was, she really made it work in her favor.

Hannah said quietly, "What are you doing to me? I feel like I'm on drugs. This all feels so good."

"Beautiful girl, don't let your relaxed body write checks your uptight mind won't let it cash." I squeezed her earlobes particularly long and hard between my thumbs and middle fingers until Hannah looked like she was about to protest and then backed off just before the sensation went over the edge in the wrong direction.

"Oooohhh. My God. Please..."

"Please what, baby?" I encouraged her to express herself.

"Why does that feel so good? So confusingly good." Then she erupted with the sexiest laugh I'd ever heard in my life. "I feel... I feel... I don't know what this is going on inside my belly, but something with you rubbing my ears. Oh, wait a second!"

She tried to push off my lap and sit up, but I saw her realization coming and headed her off at the pass. I knew eventually she would put the pieces together and realize she was aroused—that I was arousing her by rubbing her. That I had knowingly chosen that part of her body with the intention of getting her hot and bothered. Now I just had to wait and see what she would do with the results.

From the onset, I resigned myself to just being a spectator of the Hannah Farsey hormone parade. At least for tonight, anyway. Once she and I got to know each other better, I hoped like hell that would change.

I wouldn't be on the sidewalk watching the parade go by. I'd be the motherfucking grand marshal.

Finally, after at least two minutes of silence, I gave in and asked, "Are you angry?" I couldn't read her expression, and the quiet was making my skin crawl.

The silent treatment was one of my father's favorite tactics when I was a young boy and a telltale sign one of his storms of fury was brewing. That building silence was almost worse than the chaos that would surely follow.

"No. I'm not mad. I've had a really nice night with you. Thank you for making me feel good. My shoulder doesn't hurt in the slightest, so that's a win." Her accompanying smile bordered between genuine and not, and I just didn't know her well enough to understand what was driving the reaction.

"Ms. Farsey, I will rub your body every single time you let me."

She narrowed her eyes at me while pressing her lips together.

"What is this look?" I chuckled with the question, trying to keep my rising frustration at bay.

"You're a little too good—at everything—for my own safety, I think."

I couldn't help it. I tossed my head back and laughed fully. For one thing, I was so glad she wasn't mad and our night wasn't going to end in an argument. Secondly, Hannah was refreshingly honest. It wasn't something I came across very often in a woman, and I liked it.

I liked her.

I liked her a lot more than I expected to, in fact. Now I just had to get with Sebastian and Grant and see about solving this problem on our hands before I ended up falling in love.

CHAPTER FOUR

HANNAH

"What time do you think you'll be home tonight?" I asked Elijah when he pulled up alongside my car in the lot of Abstract Catering's prep kitchen the next morning.

"I'm not sure. I usually have to see what the big man has planned first. Do you need me for something?"

"Well . . ." I took a fortifying breath because I wasn't really sure how bossy he was going to be about what I was about to tell him. After the nice night we had, I wanted to believe we made headway in some sort of friendship. Harmony in our cohabitation at least.

"Today, Ms. Farsey. I'm expected to show up for my own employer this morning as well," Elijah said while typing impatiently on the laptop perched on his leg. He wore a gorgeous linen suit this morning, and somehow the slacks didn't have a single wrinkle in sight. The jacket hung neatly on a cedar hanger, gently swaying on a hook over the other door's window.

"You know what? Never mind." I wasn't used to being spoken to like this, and I didn't appreciate it. Whether it was part of his normal Neanderthal charm or not, I didn't ask for all this crap. No, all this crap was dumped into my lap, but everyone was conveniently forgetting that little fact.

It seemed like as long as I was quietly going along with this rude man's harebrained idea, no one even bothered to call and check on me. Not even Rio, who I thought was supposed to be my friend. I repeatedly reminded myself she didn't actually know what was going on between Elijah and me, but she saw us at that pool party. How could a few low spoken words from her boyfriend be enough to put her mind at ease? And now they were all expecting me to act the same way, even though it went against every truth I knew about myself. I would've thought Rio understood at least a degree of that about me too.

Honestly, my feelings were a little raw on the issue all around, and I'd stewed about it my entire shower that morning. Not calling in sick was a real feat, but that wasn't the way I was raised. I rolled my eyes so grandly at that thought, there was legitimate danger of them getting stuck with just the whites showing. It was so tiring always doing what everyone expected of me. When would I get to live my life on my terms?

Well, whether I managed to actually still show up early for the shift I wanted to bail on completely or not, I definitely didn't have time for a pity party. I always told people I was an overachiever, but even I knew the less popular doormat twin sister of that one was sucker. And I also knew which one I saw when I looked in the mirror every day.

These were the thoughts fueling my power walk across the parking lot to the side door of the kitchen. If Elijah had his driver do donuts in the lot beside me, I wouldn't have known because I was so caught up in my own bullshit. No surprise, then, when my stunning keeper appeared by my side and snatched my keys from my fingers as I tried putting the largest one in the lock.

"What do you think you're doing?" I asked through gritted

teeth and grabbed my keys back from him. It was only by luck that I got them back.

With his much taller body, he pressed in very close to my side and bent over me as though shielding me from a storm. When I went to push him away, he grabbed my hand with some unexpected maneuver that made me lose all the strength in my fingers. His grip didn't hurt but made my hand completely useless. The keys fell from my grasp and hit the concrete step with a metallic clatter. In the quiet, early morning, the piercing sound bounced off the other buildings in the business park.

"Do you remember the rules we discussed on day one, beautiful?"

I chose to stare at the center of his chest rather than answer him. I was pretty sure if I had to discuss his damn rules one more time, I'd first knee him in the balls and then recite the law and order of Elijah Banks to his crumpled frame.

"No, I'm sorry, I don't recall agreeing to any such thing. Must've been one of your halfwit sleepover guests."

"Ahhh, see, that's where you're wrong already."

"Oh, my bad. They're quarter-wit? You should aim higher, master."

He threw his head back and laughed, and I was enraged. This guy was really pissing me off this morning.

"No, baby. I don't have sleepover guests."

"One," I announced emphatically, hearing my voice gaining gusto, "don't call me baby. Two, get out of my way. I need to get my day started, or lunch won't be ready in time." When I pushed him back with my hand on his lower abdomen, I was shocked by how firm it was. But given the amount of swimming he did and the healthy food I saw in the house, it made sense.

Elijah circled his long fingers around my wrist while I stooped down to pick up my keys. When I rose to stand, he didn't let go. I pulled once, and he widened his eyes.

"Let. Go."

In a lethally calm, quiet voice, he issued, "We'll talk after work tonight. There won't be a repeat of this kind of behavior. Ever. If those sick motherfuckers have this place staked out right now, they're seeing your bratty behavior. If you were really mine, you'd be on your knees right now, begging for forgiveness. In one way or another."

His hazel eyes danced closer to silver while he practically stroked me to orgasm with the potent combination of his words and promising stare. Thank God when I spoke my voice came out steady, although the usually husky tone sounded like I had dry toast for breakfast and nothing to wash it down.

"You're crazy, man. Seriously." I paused a moment to gulp down some much-needed air and then added, "But that does circle us back to how this whole shit show started. I was going to tell you I won't be home tonight."

"That's not how this works, my beauty."

"Haaan. Naaa. My name is Hannah. And I don't know what you're talking about. How what works?"

Clearly, I had to get better at anticipating this man's lightning-fast movements. Before I could make sense of what happened, he had my braid wrapped around his fist and my head cranked back at such an intense angle he could examine my tonsils if he wanted. Delicious sparks of arousal licked across my skin and whipped into a frenzy between my thighs. Elijah inched his lips closer to mine, and when I did nothing to protest, he inched closer still.

We were nearly touching when he finally growled,

"When you want something, or when you want to go somewhere, you ask me first. You do not make arrangements and then tell me about it after the fact. Do you understand?"

"You're not—"

"Yes or no, beauty. Do. You. Understand?"

"This is not—"

His hungry and much-too-quick kiss stole my protesting words and every other remaining feeble comeback I had at the ready. His full lips felt as velvety as I'd imagined they would. Even though there was only the press of his lips to mine—no tongue, nibbles, sucking, buildup or cool down of any type—I was instantly breathless.

Holy shit. Elijah Banks was a dangerous man. Dangerous to my sanity, physical well-being, sexual stability, and everything else I could think of.

Finally, he released my hair but held firmly to each arm, just above my elbows. This time I was grateful for the bondage because my head was twirling with arousal and my sense of balance was completely thrown off.

"Now, what did you want to ask me?" he asked with that sexy grin.

After a steadying inhale, I stammered, "I . . . I have to go by my house to pick up some things. There's no way I'll get away without staying for dinner, maybe cards or board games. Just depends who's around while I'm there."

Elijah straightened my chef's coat while he answered, "Then I'll join you."

"You weren't invited."

He tilted his head, and his freshly fucked–looking hair flopped to one side. How did he look so put together yet so sinfully disheveled?

"So we're good?" I was gaining a bit of my spine back as I opened the door to go inside. I had to get my day started, and I had to put space between this man and me if that was ever going to happen.

"Thanks for understanding. Have a great day at work." I gave him my fake competitive cheer smile. "Don't wait up. Like I said, I might be home late. If at all."

"Hannah. I'm warning you now."

"You know what, Elijah?" I stepped inside the kitchen and surreptitiously engaged the lock so when the door closed, he wouldn't be able to open it again. "I don't really care. Buh-bye." Then I closed the door in his ridiculously handsome face with a solid *whump*.

By the time Rio arrived about two hours later, I had made all the planned lunch menu items and my grandmother's pie dough. Perfectly round balls were covered and chilling in the walk-in, awaiting their fate.

"What is all this?" she asked as she came out of the cooler and saw the inventory. "Someone was working off some steam. Who do I need to steer clear of?" She was grinning from ear to ear because only another chef would recognize that much dough for what it really was.

Working out one's anger the old-fashioned way.

I gave a stilted wave, signaling that I was the guilty party. Although when it came to making pie crust from scratch, was anyone really guilty?

Rio shook her head slowly from side to side while chuckling. "I knew that bastard would be a nightmare to live with. I'm so sorry, honey."

After giving me a longer survey, she asked quietly, "Do you need to talk? Outside? Or better yet, do I need to do the lunch deliveries for you today and serve him his balls instead of what he ordered?"

When I'd gotten dressed this morning, I planned for my turn at lunch deliveries by wearing my tennis shoes instead of my usual kitchen clogs. We rotated the chore through the staff so no one got burned out. But with all the drama that went on when I first arrived, I had forgotten what that meant.

I'd be seeing my sexy landlord sooner than I thought.

"Can you help me get some supplies out of my car?" Rio asked, her voice a bit louder than it had just been. Clearly this question was more for show for the other staff.

"Sure. Lead the way, boss." I tried for my normally upbeat attitude instead of the sour one I'd been nursing so far. I was pretty sure the others had noticed I wasn't myself, because everyone was giving me a pretty wide berth.

When we were far enough from the building, Rio asked, "What's going on, my friend?"

"Not much. What's up with you?" I tried to keep my smile as real as possible. Rio's bullshit meter was a finely tuned piece of equipment, and I knew I wouldn't get away with faking it.

"Cut the crap, Hannah. There's enough pie crust dough in our walk-in to supply Julian at Thanksgiving. I know it's that glowing-eyed motherfucker you're bowing down to that's the problem. Now out with it."

"Nah, I can handle him."

Rio stopped in her tracks and faced me. "Mama, I'm worried about you, and you aren't making it easier by protecting him."

"I promise, the minute he starts getting to me—in a bad way—you'll be my phone-a-friend."

"Promise? Because Elijah Banks gets under my skin

quicker than anyone I've ever known." She gave me a wry smile and then continued. "And that's saying a lot. I mean, shit, you saw the Abbigail onslaught, did you not?"

"I promise. But boy, you make a good point there. You do know a lot about aggravating people from your past dealings with Abbi," I agreed.

Yes. Change the subject. Change the subject. Change the subject.

"And she grew into that little beast. She wasn't always like that, mind you. She was this doe-eyed teenager when she moved to California. I mean, the crying thing"—Rio waved her hand through the air—"shit, that was always part of her. But the tyrant thing? That's a whole new development since she pulled up to Casa Shark."

"Really? That's so odd to me." Now I was truly invested in this topic.

"Why?"

"I don't know." I shrugged. "It seems like such a natural fit for her." I slapped my hand over my mouth, not believing I had just said that out loud. What the hell had gotten into me? I never talked about other people like that, let alone my boss. "Oh my God, Rio. I'm so sorry. I shouldn't have said that."

She just laughed. "Why not? It's the truth."

"Regardless. She's your sister-in-law and one of my bosses. It's just mean. And I'm not a mean person." Under my breath I added, "Well, not usually, anyway."

"Do you want to tell me what's going on in Malibu these days?" she prodded.

"Seriously, it's not worth the time or the oxygen it would take. It was just some high-handed bossy crap he pulled this morning. It pissed me off. And ..."

But I trailed off. I wanted to say more, I wanted to talk with Rio about the parts of what was going on with Elijah that I liked. The things about him I didn't quite understand, but I knew my body well enough to know when something felt good.

And that man definitely knew how to make me feel good.

"And what? I can tell there's more you want to say. Why not just say it? You might feel better once you get it out of your head."

"I don't know. I don't really know how to word it." We both leaned against the back of her little car. "I think I'm confused more than anything. And that doesn't make a lot of sense in itself. I'm not used to being so all over the place emotionally, or physically, for that matter. I don't like it." I paused a few beats and then just rambled, "And if my parents catch even the slightest hint of what's going on ... Oh shit, girl. You have no idea how disappointed they will be. They did not raise their daughters to be pushed around by a man, you know?"

"Wait." Rio jacked up to stand from the Fiat. "Wait a damn second."

"What?"

Oh shit. Did I say too much? Did I blow our cover?

My friend took both my hands in hers and squeezed them. The woman had a fierce grip for someone so small. "What do you mean pushed around? Has Elijah hit you or hurt you in any way? So help me—"

"No, no! I shouldn't have said it like that. I'm sorry. But you know how other people see this sort of thing, right? I'm assuming you do this? You and Mr. Twombley have this sort of relationship?"

"Hell no. Be serious."

"What do you mean, be serious?"

"From what you know of me, Hannah, can you imagine me taking orders from a man?" She rolled her eyes and said, "Oh my God, that's actually funny."

"But I thought I totally got the same vibe." I waved my hand through the air, so out of my element here, even on the verbiage of what was going on or supposed to be going on between Mr. Hottie and me. "Or whatever, from Mr. Twombley, that I do from Elijah."

"Honey, you can call him Grant. And don't get me wrong. That tree is the most dominant redwood in the forest. But living in a D/s relationship? I'm just not cut out for that. I'd never be able to sit down."

"I'm not following. What do you mean?"

"Oh boy." She laughed. "You will." She patted my back in a motherly way. "You must not have pissed him off yet."

"Ooohhh, I wouldn't say that." I kicked at the ground, thinking about my parting shots that morning before I locked him out. "I was pretty snotty to him when he dropped me off today. I all but threw him off the property."

"Damn it!" my boss shouted, and I jumped a bit from the outburst. "I have to start getting in here earlier. I'm missing all the good stuff."

"Well, now I'm dreading seeing him on the lunch deliveries. If I'm lucky, he won't be in the office today."

"Well, let's go see if his name is on the list." Rio hooked her arm in mine, and we turned toward the building.

We met each other's stare for a brief moment and then took off running across the parking lot, giggling like schoolgirls the entire way. It felt so good to laugh and release the tension of the morning and have some girl time with my friend to boot.

I was so thankful I had this woman in my life. When she

and Abbi hired me, I had no idea we'd become friends, but I was so grateful we had. Even though the shit storm currently clouding the usually sunny skies of my life was because of the exact same reason.

Sure enough, Elijah was on the delivery schedule for lunch. I thought about changing with one of my coworkers, but what good would it do? If he was still pissed at me at lunch, he'd likely still be pissed when I got home later tonight. Something told me this guy didn't let anything slip through the cracks. So I might as well take my medicine like a big girl and get it over with.

"Hey, Hannah," one of my coworkers, Brinn, called to me when we came inside. "Your phone's been pinging over there where you left it. In case you were expecting a call or whatever."

"Oh, okay. Thank you." I smiled brightly at the other staff member. For the first time today, it didn't feel like I had to concentrate to make the expression.

I checked my phone quickly before washing my hands and getting back to work. Soon, I'd have to get the van loaded and head downtown.

The message was from Elijah, and while I wanted to pretend I didn't know what he was talking about, I'd read enough naughty books and heard enough stories about friends' bedroom escapades that were much more adventurous than the handful of vanilla experiences I'd had.

Make sure you bring something extra soft to sit on for your drive back to the kitchen today. After that stunt this morning, you're going to need it.

I quickly looked up to make sure no one was watching me and then reread his message. Twice.

"Jesus Christ," I muttered and stowed my phone in the pocket of my chef's coat. Thankfully all the cooking I had to do for the morning was already done. There was no way I'd be able to concentrate on a recipe after reading that. My face had to be as red as the radishes Jorge was artfully carving into roses on the other side of the stainless-steel counter, though, because I could feel the intense heat radiating from my cheeks.

Time for a redirect on all this energy. Like . . . immediately.

"All right, fancy pants. Show me how to do this." I playfully bumped the young sous chef's hip with mine as I issued my demand. "You can't be the only one around here with this mad skill."

I spent the next hour trying to learn the new technique from my teammate. While I was great at creating new recipes because of my refined palate, knife skills like Jorge's were something I always envied. My desire to learn and the repetitive nature of the task he was teaching me helped the time pass quickly and kept my mind completely occupied.

Before I realized the time, Rio was shouting across the kitchen, "Let's get the van loaded up. We can't keep our hangry customers waiting, people!"

Jorge leaned closer while scooping radish trimmings into his garbage bowl. "Is it me, or is she unusually loud for someone so small?"

We both laughed, and I thanked him for the food art lesson before hustling into the walk-in refrigerator to start loading the cold entrées into the coolers.

The moment I got behind the wheel of the Econoline van, a certain hazel-eyed hottie came right back into sharp focus. At the first red light, which was less than a mile from the kitchen, I already had my head pressed to the center of the oversized steering wheel while I tried to get a grip on my racing heart.

"Jesus Christ," I muttered for the second time this morning. Maybe a call to one of my sisters would help distract me. If it was closing in on lunchtime, Agatha might be available for a quick chat. With my phone connected to the vehicle via Bluetooth, I used voice commands and dialed my sister.

"Hey, Hannibal, what's going on? You okay?" my sister asked, using one of a dozen nicknames my family had for me.

"Hi, sister. Yeah, I'm good. Why?" I smiled while greeting her. Just hearing one of my siblings' voices was as good as getting a warm hug from them.

"Why what?" she bounced back.

"Why did you ask if I'm okay?" Right out of the gate, too. I chuckled, trying to sound easy and breezy like I hoped I normally sounded.

"You don't normally call me in the middle of the day, Hannah."

"True. But all's well. I'm driving into downtown, so I have some windshield time. Thought I'd say hi. I haven't seen you for a few days, so I thought I'd check in with you."

"How very big sister of you," Agatha said, and I could hear the smile in her words.

"Well, that's me. Your big sister."

"So, what's going on with you? Mom said you're staying with a friend or something when I asked why you weren't at dinner."

"Yeah, it's more of a house-sitting thing. More or less." God, I was the worst liar on the planet.

"Wow, you're so full of shit. Now you have to tell me what's going on," she pressed.

"Dah, what are you talking about?" I tried to play dumb but knew the likelihood of getting away with it was slim.

Just like I had a handful of nicknames, so did my sister. We all did, actually. When my parents brought Agatha home from the hospital, I was a babbling toddler—just barely two years old. The name Agatha was impossible to pronounce for a child so young, but my parents tell the story that I immediately picked up on the similarity to my favorite showboating saying, *ta-dah!*

So, to this day, we all still call Agatha Ta-Dah, and sometimes the even shorter version, Dah.

"So, your friend must be a man, then?"

Just tell her. Just tell her. Just tell her.

"A man lives in the house I'm looking after, yes. Is that so unusual?" I asked, or defended, probably depending on whose ears you were hearing the conversation through.

"No, of course not. The unusual part is why you're not being honest with me, Hannah."

"Can we make a deal?" I asked my sister, crawling along in traffic. There had to be an accident somewhere up ahead. LA traffic always sucked, but it wasn't normally this congested in the late-morning hours.

"Yes, of course we can. I'm always here for you, you know that."

Without a moment's hesitation I responded, "Just like I would be for you."

"I know," Agatha said quietly. Her voice had the same alto pitch mine did. Our mother gave us the unique vocal gift.

"I have a feeling I'm going to need someone to talk to

over the next few weeks. Someone I can trust and who won't judge me. You've always been good in that role, Agatha. But you have to promise me a few things." I waited for her reply because I knew I had just laid out a bunch of things she would naturally want to explore. She and I were similar in so many ways, and being naturally inquisitive, almost to our detriment, was another one of those ways.

"Hanny, what have you gotten yourself into? You're freaking me out," my sister said, gaining volume with her distress.

"No, it's nothing bad, or illegal, I promise. I just know Mom and Dad will completely freak out and disapprove." I paused again, but the conversational gap wasn't for her this time. I needed to organize my thoughts better, and since I couldn't see her face and have that visual feedback to gauge if I was expressing myself clearly, I didn't want to say something I didn't first think through. And now, this whole conversation had taken an unexpected turn. I didn't call Agatha intending to confide in her specifically about what was happening in Malibu. I just wanted to hear a comforting voice and settle my ragged nerves before I saw my landlord on his turf.

"Did I lose you? Hannah?" Agatha queried.

"I'm here. Just thinking." I took a calming breath and said, "I want to do something for myself for once. I'm so tired of living my life for everyone else." I waited for a few seconds and exhaled loudly when she didn't say anything. "Does that make sense?"

"Of course, it does. I don't know why you've always thought you had to be Dana Do-Right. You deserve to live a little, girl. Hell! You deserve to live a lot! I think we all should be following in Clemmy's footsteps more often." She chuckled the last part.

"I know, right? She's seventeen—"

"Almost eighteen!" Agatha barked the interruption the way our youngest sister always did when someone spoke of her age. She made the comment with such unerring accuracy, we both burst out laughing until we were snorting on our inhalations.

"Oh my God. You know she would've stomped off in a fit by now if she heard us, right?" I asked, wiping a tear from the outer corner of my eye.

"Well, good thing she didn't hear us, then, isn't it?"

"Yes! It definitely is. God, that felt so good to laugh like that. Okay, I'm finally here at my first stop. Thank you for talking to me, Ta-Dah. I don't know what I'd do without you."

"But you didn't finish what you were saying!" my sister whined.

"You got most of it," I reassured her.

"I don't think I got any of it. Because none of it makes sense. Well, wait, not true. I understand about wanting to live your life for you. But, Han? That's the way you're supposed to live. Only you think otherwise. Well, you and the other great martyrs of the world."

"I'm going to pretend I didn't hear that martyr comment. Are you going to be home tonight? I have to come by and get some of my stuff. If we can get some privacy in that circus tent we call a home, I'll fill you in the best I can. Okay? I really have to go, or there are going to be a lot of hungry, spoiled rich dudes and dudettes calling my boss to complain." I stuffed my phone and keys in my emergency pack disguised as a great crossbody bag and slung it over my head while I tried to say goodbye.

But Agatha had one more comment. "I don't know when you're going to quit working for other people and strike out on your own. You're so talented, Hannah. You need to open a restaurant."

"Blah blah blah."

"Hannibal?"

"Yeah?" I asked.

"I'm glad you called me. I love you."

"I love you too, Dah. I'll see you later."

"Bye."

With a much lighter heart and clearer mind, I loaded the lunches onto the cart and headed into Shark Enterprises.

CHAPTER FIVE

ELIJAH

My executive assistant, Carmen, buzzed the intercom feature on my desk phone.

"Yes?" I asked the young man.

"Security called with the information you asked for. It is Ms. Farsey who is making the lunch deliveries today. I made sure you were on the recipient list like you asked. I checked twice, so there should be no mistake."

"You're a good man, Carmen. I don't care what everyone else says." We both chuckled because he recognized my comment for the joke it was. The guy had been with me long enough to know my dry sense of humor, and he often gave it right back.

Now I just had to bide my time until she got to my office. Normally they started up here on the top floor and worked their way down to the first floor, but I wasn't sure how vindictive my beauty was going to be.

I wasn't a regular partaker of the service like Bas and Grant because many more of my day's appointments were out in the field, but when I looked at the schedule on Abstract's server late last night and saw Hannah would be making the deliveries, I added myself to the list.

It was just a stroke of luck that she chose to behave the

way she did when I escorted her to work this morning. Now, if my luck continued, she'd walk out of here with a nice red ass, and my palm would tingle for the rest of the afternoon from spanking it.

I'd come up with so many filthy and creative ways to teach my new playmate a lesson. Settling on one had been a distracting challenge. Fortunately, Bas had canceled the meeting first thing this morning with Grant and me, so I'd spent a lot of time daydreaming about Hannah. I'd also relived every single moment of our evening together, which resulted in two mind-altering sessions with my fist in my office's attached bathroom.

Normally, jacking off was something I did for biology reasons only. My cock was hard and causing problems—I dealt with it. But ever since Ms. Farsey took up residence under my roof, even that changed.

Now, it was like I was a teenager again. Self-inflicted sexual challenges like seeing how long I could make myself wait before giving in to the need. Seeing how many times I could take myself to the edge before completely exploding while gasping my beauty's name from my lips. Seeing which memory took me to that edge fastest. Seeing—if I concentrated hard enough—if I could still smell the magical, mysterious redolence of her perfume or, better yet, her natural arousal... feel her butter-soft skin... taste the whisper of salt on it.

Jesus. Fucking. Christ.

It seemed like eight years ago that Twombley and I would watch Bas climb the walls until Abbigail came by with his lunch. When she'd finally arrive, he would toy with the poor girl like a cat does with a mouse before she would finally scamper away, usually in tears. Then Shark, being the bastard he was and apparently one I could totally relate to, would sit triumphantly and eat that damn meal like it was the best thing he'd ever tasted. The dude would all but lick the plate clean because her hands had touched it. When he was done, he would even take a ridiculous amount of care with the linen napkin, folding it as neatly as it was before he started.

Shit. I was going to owe him an apology for all the times I busted his balls.

Or not.

As long as I kept the storm I felt rioting in my system on the inside and didn't let anything show on the outside, I should be safe.

Because really, how could this be happening? How could I be into this little hottie already? Yes, she was gorgeous. She was smart and ambitious. I'd always found those traits to be incredibly attractive in a woman. But I swore off falling for a woman ever again. Women? Hell yes. But one singular woman? No way. Not ever again.

Ever. Again.

I could have it tattooed across my forehead for how intensely I had made the vow. Yet here I was, pacing around my office like a caged lion.

Pacing. Fucking pacing, waiting for a woman to show up at my door.

When the knock sounded, I actually jumped. I snickered at my own absurdity and quickly chalked it up to being caught up in my own thoughts. My assistant's deep voice came from the other side of the heavy wood panel.

"Mr. Banks, your lunch has arrived."

In two long strides, I was across to the door and yanking on the handle. Judging by the look on both Carmen's and Ms.

Farsey's faces, I must have looked deranged when the door swung inward and I loomed in the open frame.

"Hello," she said, and that sultry voice reached right down the front of my linen slacks and jacked my cock with tight, smoky fingers.

"Ms. Farsey. How nice to see you. Thank you, Carmen. That's everything for now. Why don't you take your lunch break, too? We'll be fine here."

"I won't take but a minute," Hannah said. "In and out, you know how this goes." She pushed the catering cart into my office fully, and I quietly closed the door on her heels. The rush of air behind her made the loose tendrils framing her heavenly face fan forward like a spray of fine silk.

"How has your day been so far? Productive, I'm guessing?" I was a wall of coiled need, trapping her between the closed door and my body.

"It— It's been fine. Yours? And where would you like your lunch? You aren't one of our regulars on this floor, so I'm not familiar with your preferences." She babbled nervously and tried to sidestep past me.

"Set the tray down, Hannah."

"Pardon?"

"Put. The food. Down." And fuck if she didn't do as I instructed. Possibly for the first time behind closed doors, she did as she was told without so much as a single argumentative word.

No, that was bullshit. It was the first time, period.

"Good girl."

"Don't speak to me that way," she demanded.

I tilted my head to the side, as if regarding her from a slightly different angle would clue me in to what she was objecting to exactly.

"You're so infuriating," she growled.

"How so?" I asked calmly, running my fingers back through my hair to push it away from my face.

"You speak to me like I'm a child, then tilt your head like that"—she demonstrated with an exaggerated ticktock of her own while she continued to chew me out—"and look so sexy it steals my breath and rational thought in the same split second. God! I want to knee you in the balls and beg for forgiveness at the same time."

She dropped her chin to cradle her face in her palms and whimpered. "I've never been so confused in my entire life, Mr. Banks. I'm starting to despise you because of it."

Maybe it was her admission that made me bold. Maybe it was the ache I felt so painfully in my balls, caused by that admission, that was giving me the courage. I had no damn clue. But something gave me the insane bravery to take a step closer to her—and then another. Until finally I skated my fingertips along the V-neck of her Abstract Catering T-shirt.

"I have never wanted to be a T-shirt so badly in my life," I rumbled.

She grinned, likely remembering the night before when I made the exact comment, only about the bubbles in her bath.

"I wouldn't have pegged you for the jealous type. But that's two comments in twenty-four hours to the contrary."

"Normally, I'm not." I continued running my fingers along the edge of the cotton top. Fantasies of ripping it in two pieces to get to the treasure beneath were assaulting my imagination.

I leaned even closer to Hannah so I could speak right into the pit of her ear. "I'm not sure what you're doing to me, Ms. Farsey, but it's maddening. And elemental." Impulsively,

I darted my tongue out and slowly licked the shell of her ear. "And intoxicating."

I pulled back to regard her expression but didn't put space between our bodies. While I wanted to gauge her reaction before continuing, I didn't—no—I *couldn't* bring myself to move away from her.

When I said this next part, I wanted to be sure she listened to my words with careful consideration. With slow, seductive, and dangerous promise on every single syllable, I confessed to my beautiful Hannah, "I want to hurt you just so I can comfort you. I want to fuck you roughly so I can make love to you sweetly. I want you to know every extreme sensation your body is capable of feeling by my hands. I want to be like a drug in your veins, girl. I want you to beg for it. Need it. Hate it and love it."

"I—umm—I—uhh—"

I couldn't help the chuckle that escaped, but judging by her immediate retreat backward, she didn't appreciate the levity. Fortunately for me, she couldn't go far.

"Hannah? Can I ask you something?"

"I—I—think so. Yeah, sure." She exhaled dramatically after finally getting out a complete sentence.

"Be honest with me when answering, please."

"All right. But then I really have to get going. I have all this to deal with." She motioned to the catering cart with a wide, sweeping hand gesture.

"Have you had sex before? With a man?"

"Not that it's any of your concern," the goddess in front of me snapped. Damn, her foul attitude turned me on.

Coolly, I replied, "Of course it's my concern."

"How do you figure?"

"Because when we fuck—and Hannah? We *will* fuck—I want to know what I'm dealing with going in."

She opened her mouth to respond and then closed it again. Opened again with a sharp inhale, maybe ready to reply with a better quip than the first time, but just as quickly snapped her lower jaw closed with a clack so loud I was concerned for the integrity of her molars.

"Now, before you scurry off, what time are we expected at your parents' tonight?" I angled my body away from hers, freeing her to move about as she wished.

"Oh, not this again. Why do you insist on antagonizing me?"

"I told you. You're not going alone."

"And I told you, you aren't invited to join me."

Distance. I needed to put some distance between our bodies or I'd have her over my lap for the discipline I'd spent the better part of the morning fantasizing about. For such an intelligent woman, she really wasn't grasping the concept of who was in charge in our relationship.

Across the room, I propped my ass on the edge of my desk and regarded her with calm patience while she found a place to set out my lunch. When ordering the meal in the wee hours of the morning, my only thought was getting to see her again in the middle of the workday.

But now that she was in front of me and carefully setting the food out as though she was caring for me personally, the moment seemed intimate. I gave my head a solid shake. Jesus Christ, was I that desperate for companionship? Was I that hard up for the genuine attention of another human that I would let paying someone to prepare a meal for me be so easily used as a substitute? I needed to get a grip, and fast. My normally tight, controlled composure was already slipping, and I'd been around this woman less than a week.

"You're not thinking rationally, Mr. Banks."

Truer words have not been spoken, beauty.

"Explain it to me, then."

"The story we decided to tell my family, if you recall, was that I'm house-sitting. Correct?" she asked with confidence. Wherever she was going with this line of thinking, she was sure she was about to score the winning goal.

"Yes. That's correct."

"If you're in town and with me when I go to my house tonight, why would I need to be house-sitting? You can't tell me that makes sense."

"Who said you were house-sitting for *me*?"

"It makes so much more sense that way. Who else would you be? I'm not in the habit of showing up for dinner with random guys in tow."

"Why wouldn't you bring home a man you're dating?"

"No way." She shook her head. "They'd never buy it."

"Why not? I can be very charming." I pushed away from my desk and stood to my full height.

"Oh, trust me, I know all about your charm," she began, but when I took one step toward her, she objected.

"No," she said, holding her arm out stiffly as if warding off someone who'd just tested positive for COVID-19. "You just stay over there. Far away from me. I wasn't joking about still needing to deliver these lunches."

My grin grew wider the more she babbled.

"Don't do the grin either, and I swear if you throw in the hair flop too, I'm not kidding… I won't come home tonight. You don't play fair. Not even a little bit."

"Whaaatt?" I laughed and ended up sputtering the word more than speaking it.

"Maybe I should start fighting fire with fire? Walk around the house in a little thong bathing suit?" A mischievous glitter danced in her blue gaze, and she came closer to me. Exactly what she had just instructed me not to do. "Tell me, Elijah," she purred, and her throaty voice had my sight narrowly focused on just her mouth.

My God, how I wanted to hear what she sounded like after choking on my cock. Or shouting through an orgasm.

"What's that, beautiful?" I asked, matching my tone to the husky seduction in hers.

"What's your favorite color?"

Silly girl. She was stoking a fire in the wrong kitchen. She'd learn the hard way, though. Years of running my mouth on the streets ensured I could verbally spar with the pros. I tilted my head with an extra bit of force, ensuring the longer strands on top fell to the side the way she'd admitted to having a weakness for, and then grinned before leaning in close so I was right beside her ear. When I spoke, she would feel my answer as well as hear it.

"Flesh."

★ ★ ★

Later that afternoon, while seated at the conference table in Sebastian's office, we waited for Jacob Cole to arrive for our meeting. Work on my best friend's lifelong dream building, the Edge, was progressing as scheduled, despite more setbacks than any of us could've predicted.

Sure, construction projects hit snags—and sometimes

came to complete grinding halts—but this one had seen its share of challenges, and it was incredible that the budget and timeline to completion hadn't been completely blown to hell.

"You should be taking more credit for this than you are," Grant said, still pacing along the wall of windows.

"How so? It's been about ten days since I've been on-site."

"Ever since a certain hot blonde moved in? Speaking of that, what did you tell Shawna? Did you have to get a restraining order?" The tall guy laughed when he asked the last question, but nothing about that topic was amusing.

Shit, if he only knew.

I shot my eyes to Bas, who had excused himself to take a phone call while we waited for the young architect to arrive. From what we could hear from this end of the conversation, he was talking to his sister, Pia.

"What's up? Why are you looking at him?"

"I just don't want him giving his opinion on this too."

"Which part?"

"All of it," I muttered. "You know how he gets about club girls. If he knew she was coming to my house, he'd launch into a twenty-minute speech about privacy and security, and Christ"—I raked my fingers back through my hair—"my ears would be bleeding by the time he was done."

"I really thought he'd lighten up once the kid got here, you know?" Grant waited for some sort of response from me, so I gave a quick dip of my chin in agreement. "But instead, I think he's wound even tighter."

"He's got more at stake now. It makes sense when you look at it from his perspective."

"You're right. I know you are. He's driving me crazy, though."

Changing topics, because I really didn't want Grant to drift back to Hannah or Shawna, I commented on the tardiness of our guest.

"This is so unlike Cole to be late. Normally the guy is waiting in reception like a faithful hound with his master's end-of-day slippers."

"I was thinking the same thing. I mean, not the eloquent simile and shit, but yeah, he's never late," Twombley said with a chuckle.

As if our conversation summoned the man, a knock sounded on the door across the suite. Grant was halfway across the room before I could offer to do the honors, but I stood to straighten my suit and properly greet our appointment.

Shark wrapped up his call, and we all congregated in the center of the office and exchanged pleasantries.

"Jacob! Nice to see you again," I said, shaking hands with the man. "How was your trip? Barcelona, wasn't it?"

"Yes, great memory, Mr. Banks," the young architect answered while shaking my hand.

"Please. We've talked about this." I sighed. "Call me Elijah."

"Elijah, right." He smiled apologetically, and it really was tough to be truly mad at the guy.

"And Grant, how are you? I understand congratulations are in order on your engagement." The two men shook hands, and we all moved deeper into the office toward the conference table.

"Thank you, Jake. Can't say I thought I'd ever be in these shoes, but they feel really good." Grant rocked back on his heels, and the smile on his face was so wide and genuine, it was hard to not smile along with my best friend.

Bas and Jake shook hands finally, and the young man jolted as though stepping barefoot on a few Legos.

"I brought something back from Spain for the new baby," he said excitedly, but then his expression fell. "But I left it in the hotel. And I hope I'm not overstepping with the gift in general."

"Dude, it's totally unnecessary," Bas said while putting his meaty hand on the guy's shoulder, "but appreciated nonetheless. And what do you mean, the hotel? You haven't found a place yet?"

It was interesting to observe Sebastian interact with Jacob this way. His physical gesture of friendship and words of concern for Cole's housing situation surprised me to the point I caught myself gawking at the exchange.

Our friend seemed to be regarding Jake in a younger brotherly way—similar to the way he acted with Pia. Of course, not nearly as intimate, because he and Jake were lacking the history he had with his actual sibling. But seeing Bas forge a relationship with someone new warmed me inside. An unidentifiable emotion filled my chest and created a tightness there that made that spot's normal oxygen and carbon dioxide exchange quite difficult.

Was this pride? Some sort of satisfaction in knowing he got to this point on his own after so many years and so many fucked-up interactions and failed attempts at relationships with people outside our small, immediate circle?

While I wanted to claim complete responsibility for Sebastian's social and emotional growth and maturity—because that was the kind of guy I was—I knew it was partly Abbigail's doing. Kaisan probably played a part in the transformation too. Even though the infant was merely a couple months on this planet, we'd seen changes in the man since he became a father.

When we settled down to work, it was clear Jake hadn't been idle while he was away. The new drawings he brought depicted the next phase of construction, and he carefully laid them out on the table's flat surface. Much like the first time we met with the talented architect, we were almost speechless.

"Wow, Jake," Grant finally said. "These are incredible." He scanned the drawings from left to right and back again and then chuckled. "I don't know where to look first."

"Well, unfortunately, I already know the first revision that will have to be made on these. The city just passed an ordinance about view obstructions at about twenty-five stories. So, these balcony overhangs will probably have to be shortened by nine to twelve inches." He took a step back and regarded his drawing from that position, and when Bas, Grant, or I didn't add anything to the conversation, he finally looked up to meet our stares.

"Is that a deal breaker?" he asked Sebastian. And I swear, if Bas had said yes, he would've marched on City Hall to have the ordinance reversed.

In lieu of an answer, my friend chuckled. He thumped Jacob on the back and squeezed the guy's shoulder to put him at ease. "No, man, it's not a deal breaker. Do what you need to do. I'm sure no one will even notice nine to twelve inches."

"Not according to Elijah," Grant mumbled but then barked out a laugh at his own ridiculous joke. The look on poor Jake's face was so comical, I couldn't hold in my own laughter then either.

"Twombley, I can't help your dick envy, man. You'd think at your height, size wouldn't be an issue, wee man," I teased.

Sebastian folded his arms across his broad chest and

pinched the bridge of his nose between his thumb and forefinger. "Jesus Christ, will you two get it together?"

The architect decided to steer us back on track, and it was probably a good thing, too, or Bas might have ruptured something vital. I was sure we'd be getting an earful when the young guy left the meeting.

"Now what are your plans for interior design? I can start putting some feelers out with my colleagues who design on this scale—"

"I already have someone hired," Bas said, cutting him off before he could finish.

"Oh. Okay. In that case, if you wouldn't mind sending me the firm's contact information so I can introduce myself and do some preliminary inquiries?"

"She may actually be in the building. If you have a few minutes, I can introduce you right now." Sebastian didn't wait for Jacob to respond before he was striding across the office to his desk. If I had to guess, he was either going to have Craig track Pia down or he had access to her calendar and would just look for himself as to her whereabouts.

When I sneaked a glance Grant's way, I found his blue gaze waiting on my inquisitive hazel one. Apparently we both had the same impression that our best friend was acting a little impatient when it came to introducing Jacob and Cassiopeia.

Then it hit me. Someone was feeling like adding matchmaker to his résumé this afternoon. Interesting.

"Jacob." I offered my hand to the talented man. "Great work, as usual. Unfortunately, I have to head to my next appointment. I look forward to seeing you soon, though." We shook hands, and Grant used the same excuse and was out Bas's door on my heels. He probably didn't want to face our buddy's wrath alone, so whether he had an appointment or not, he was having his exit visa stamped at the same time.

Out in the hall, I smacked him in the taut abdomen with the back of my hand. "Dick. You know he's not going to drop that shit."

"You have to admit it was funny though," Grant said, grinning.

"Yeah, it was. But what the hell with Pia? Do you think our boy is trying to fix them up?"

"That's what I was thinking. Cole is a baby, though. Pia would chew a guy like that up and spit him out before the dude even knew what hit him."

"Truth, my brother. It would be really fun to watch, though, wouldn't it?"

We both laughed then, even louder than we should've at Jacob Cole's expense. He really was a good guy.

When Grant was quiet for too long, I looked up to see a wistful expression on his face.

"What?"

"Hmmm?"

"Where'd you go just then?"

"I was just thinking that it would be really nice to see her happy. She deserves it, you know?"

"I couldn't agree with you more, man."

CHAPTER SIX

HANNAH

After parking on the circular driveway of my parents'
Brentwood home, I checked my rearview mirror one more
time. I wasn't completely convinced Elijah wouldn't show up
for dinner, despite the multitude of ways I uninvited him. It
was oddly comforting, though, to see the dark SUV creep down
the street past our address after I made the sharp left turn into
the driveway.

From what Elijah had said that first day at Abstract,
when he and Grant came over to gather the details about what
happened to me, several of his men would be protecting my
family around the clock. Whether it should or not, it warmed
my heart to know he was a man of his word.

It was probably foolish to think his integrity had anything
to do with me personally and wasn't just his dedication to
Grant and ultimately Abbigail's man, Sebastian Shark, but
I couldn't help feeling the way I did. And with every day that
passed, every interaction we shared, the feelings were getting
more and more difficult to keep separated.

I still hadn't confided in my sexy protector, but the
nightmares stemming from the day I was filmed in the walk-in
cooler hadn't let up. He had asked me about it the first two or
three mornings I woke up in his beautiful oceanside home, but

he let it go after that. Undoubtedly, a stern lecture would be coming my way after my confession, and the longer I let the problem persist, I assumed the bigger the punishment would be.

Also, I received the third call from an unknown number today. As was the case with the previous two calls, I was promptly hung up on, only to be left staring at the blank display on my cell phone and feeling the familiar icy fingers of anxiety gripping me around the throat until I nearly passed out. So, yeah, I knew I was going to have to come clean about the phone calls too. Mr. Banks was not going to be a happy landlord, for sure.

Eventually I would have to discuss my past with the man too. But that was a big, smelly pile of crap I would leave buried for as long as possible. Plus, there was no telling how long I would have to be in Elijah's proximity. They could very well figure out who was causing all these problems for the businessmen, and I'd be out of harm's way and be able to come home.

With one last check of my hair, I made myself a promise. If I was still staying at the Banks Estate in a week, I would talk to the man about my situation. Because there was one thing I knew about my history—it always came back to haunt me. Usually at the worst times and with unerring clarity to those around me. Then I always wished I had been the one who had brought it up first.

So maybe this should be the first time in my life that I was in control of both my anxiety and what caused it in the first place. I had just said to Agatha today that I wanted to start living my life for myself instead of feeling like I was living for everyone else. What better way than to take the bull by the horns?

"There's my Hannah Banana!" my father said when I walked into the family room. He was in his customary spot in front of the television, with the local station's evening edition of the daily news playing at a volume much too loud for everyone else's pleasure.

"Hi, Daddy." I smiled, bending over to hug him in his chair so he wouldn't have to stand. The man worked too hard, and if it was a mercy I could show him, then so be it.

"Daddy, this is so loud . . . Can you not hear it, or are you trying to drown out Clemson's music again?"

"Is that noise considered music these days?" He rolled his eyes, and I playfully shoved his shoulder. He used to say the same thing about the music I played at her age and every one of my sisters since. Funny thing, when he thought no one was around, I'd hear him humming those same songs with incredible accuracy.

"Mark, she's listening to Led Zeppelin. You've told all the girls too many stories about your glory days at this point to try to pretend you don't like Robert Plant," my mom teased as she bustled through the great room with a laundry basket perched on her hip.

"Hello, beautiful daughter," she said to me warmly and thrust her cheek out for a kiss. I swept the basket out of her arms first and then gave her the kiss she was hoping for.

"Let me take this from you. The other girls can help around here too, you know. Is Ta-Dah home? I didn't see her car in the driveway," I asked, balancing the laundry basket on the back of the sofa. I really hoped we could finish our conversation from that afternoon.

Just then, Sheppard, my twenty-two-year-old sister, beelined through. She must have caught my question. "Do any of you read the family chat? Why do we even have it if no one reads it?"

"Sheppard, honey, please answer your sister if you know the information," my mother said with the patience of a saint. "Hannah can't have her phone out most of the day while she's working. She's explained that to all of us a number of times."

My sister heaved an exaggerated sigh and said, "She texted and said traffic was really bad and she was running late."

"Now was that so difficult?" my father asked.

"I just don't know why you and Mom insisted we create that text thread if we aren't going to utilize it."

"Sheppard, I'm not going to warn you again about this nonsense," my dad said, and I swiftly moved the laundry basket to the floor and went to my sister's side.

Close to her ear, I muttered, "Don't get him riled up, Shep. His heart. Okay? Just walk away, please. If you really need someone to argue with tonight, I'll come in your room and you can lay into me. But please don't get on Daddy's nerves."

"You must get really tired, Hannah," Shep bit, not even trying to keep the conversation between just us anymore.

"Pardon?" I looked at her, confused.

"Carrying the weight of the world. Righting all the wrongs and so on. I mean, seriously, sister. What's next? World peace? Curing cancer?"

"Unnecessary, Sheppard. So unnecessary. You're exceptionally nasty this evening, and it has nothing to do with me or our parents. Maybe you should go to your room until dinner is ready?"

"No, I'm leaving. I have a spin class in twenty minutes."

We just stared at each other for a few tense moments before I finally pulled her into a hug. Or whatever you called a one-sided embrace, because she just let her arms hang limply by her sides. I couldn't help but notice how I felt more bones than anything else in that hug.

"Please drive safely. I love you, Shep."

"Yeah, whatever." And my ill-tempered younger sister snatched her car keys off the row of hooks by the door between the house and garage and was gone.

The entire house collectively exhaled when we heard the weather seal at the base of the garage door make contact with the concrete floor once she was gone.

In silence, I picked up the laundry basket and went to my room to fold the clothes for my mom and pull myself together. My younger sister was becoming increasingly ill-tempered, and I had no idea what was causing it. I'd have to talk to Agatha when she got home and see if she had any insight. My personality had always been at odds with Sheppard's, but the things she said tonight were downright hurtful. Intentionally so. We weren't taught to treat one another that way, and I couldn't understand what I'd done to make her so hateful.

Tears were trying their best to make a predinner appearance, but I took some calming breaths to banish the emotional onslaught. After the third cycle of ins and outs, I heard my mom clear her throat in my doorway.

"Han, I'm so sorry, honey. I don't know what gets into her sometimes, but you didn't deserve that."

"I know that, Mom. She's out of control, though. Do you need help with dinner? I'm sorry I didn't get here sooner."

"Don't be silly. You cook all day. I'm sure it's the last thing you want to do when you get home."

"It's different when I'm cooking for you guys. Well, you guys minus Sheppard."

"Hannah. Rochelle."

"What?"

We both laughed before she folded me into the best mom hug I'd had in a while. Somehow, she always knew when I needed one of her professional-grade embraces. Apparently after raising five children, certain things became second nature.

"I'm going to finish folding this before dinner. Plus, I'm enjoying the quiet in here," I told my mom when she headed out of my bedroom. Something about a girl's childhood sanctuary could still bring solace, even at my age. I didn't have teen boy idol posters hanging above my bed anymore, or garish pink-and-purple wallpaper, but if these walls could talk, they would really embarrass me. Especially if a certain hazel-eyed sex devil was the one doing the interrogating.

Forgetting about the laundry now that he was in the foreground of my thoughts again, I flopped down on my bed and stared at the ceiling. I wondered if Elijah would like to go ballooning with me. I wondered if I was still allowed to do that. I remembered the initial set of house rules stated I could do whatever I wanted as long as I let him know my plans in advance. I laughed out loud, picturing him afraid of heights and finally finding the man's Achilles' heel. Oh, to have a bargaining chip to use against him.

Yes! I would bring it up tonight, or maybe I'd let him drive me to the kitchen in the morning so we could talk about it then.

"What are you thinking about?"

"Aaahhh!" I shouted when my sister Agatha caught me in the middle of my reverie. I knew I had the goofiest grin on my face as my sibling found me in a daze much more pleasant than the disaster of reality she'd narrowly escaped in our home.

She raised her finger as if hailing the bartender at our favorite watering hole at the Standard in the Financial District. Anytime we needed to let our hair down a little bit, that was where we went.

"Joaquin, I'll have what she's having," she shouted, still playacting with her voice as loud as necessary to be heard in a crowded bar.

I hopped up from my bed and went to stand beside her, getting in on the silliness. It was exactly what I needed. "Tall, icy hazel eyes, and sexy as fuck. Better make it a double tonight, Joaquin."

Agatha slowly looked across her shoulder to me and then back to the pretend Joaquin. "I better get mine to go. And hurry up, will ya?" She poured on an obnoxious accent of some sort, and I sputtered the start of a laugh but quickly sealed my lips when she dealt me a sidelong glare. With eyes forward again, my sister said in her loud, rude accent, "I'm not gettin' any younger here!"

In a fit of giggles, we embraced and fell onto my bed in each other's arms. It didn't matter that we were an average age of twenty-five and laughing so hard we had tears rolling down our cheeks. It didn't matter that our dad had to call to us at least twice from my doorway to let us know dinner was ready. It especially didn't matter that less than an hour before, tears were threatening to run down my cheeks for a completely different reason.

All that mattered was Agatha Christine Farsey was one of the best friends I had in this entire world. And what was even better than that?

No. The only thing that mattered right here and right now was this amazing, perfect woman was my sister.

"What's gotten into the two of you?" Our dad chuckled as he stood and watched us straighten our clothes and wipe our tear-streaked cheeks.

"Just letting off a little steam being silly, Daddy," Agatha explained and stood on her tippy toes to kiss his cheek when he bent forward to meet her halfway. Our dad was a tall man at six feet three inches, and this particular sister was the shortest of the brood at an exact foot shorter than he was.

The three of us strolled toward the kitchen, and delicious aromas assaulted my senses. Everything smelled better—and tasted better—when you didn't have to prepare it yourself.

"It's too bad your other sister doesn't just lighten up. I don't know what got into her tonight, Hannah, but you didn't deserve any of that. You know that, right?"

"Of course I do, Daddy. She must be under a lot of pressure at school or something."

"Don't make excuses for her. She doesn't deserve your mercy all the time. She doesn't deserve it from any of us at this point, and I'm wondering if that's why she's so nasty to everyone. Because she gets away with it. Your mother and I did not tolerate you girls treating each other that way when you were younger, so I don't know what makes her think it's okay now. This is still my home. My rules."

My dad's voice had gotten increasingly louder as we walked into the kitchen, where my mom was setting the last serving dish on the table. My youngest sister, Clemson, was filling everyone's water glasses from a large pitcher.

"Daddy, don't get upset. Please." I rubbed up and down on his forearm. "You know it's not good for you. I can handle Shep. Seriously, please don't give it another thought." A redirect was in order, and the steaming dishes on the table were the perfect relief.

"Mom, everything looks delicious as usual. And hello, favorite youngest sister." I intercepted Clemson before she could walk past and kissed her fresh-faced cheek. "How was practice?"

"Epic," she said, grinning widely. "Shaved an entire second off my backstroke split."

"Good job, you! Here, you have first crack at the meat and potatoes for that achievement," I said enthusiastically and thrust the bowl of mashed potatoes toward her. "You must be starving."

I watched in awe as she piled her plate full of my mom's homemade meatloaf and then smothered it with the rich gravy she made from the greasy pan drippings.

"Mom, I was thinking about this meal the entire practice," Clemson said around a bite of protein.

"Well, in that case, next time you text me after school, I'm going to tell you it's a surprise so you aren't tortured for three hours."

Clemmy put her hands over the center of her chest and gasped. "You wouldn't."

We all chuckled at her antics. Then I asked, "Do you have a meet this weekend? I haven't been able to catch one lately."

"Yeah, on Saturday. That would be great if you'd come, Hannibal. And you haven't seen the new aquatics center since they finished it. You won't believe how different it looks from the old pool you used to swim in."

"I'd really like that. Text me the details, and I'll do my best to get down there."

"Absolutely."

As we finished dinner, Sheppard came home. Instead of joining the family in the kitchen, she stormed through and went straight to her room.

With my dishes in the sink, I turned to say good night to my family. "I'm going to head out, you guys. Thank you for dinner, Mom. I love you all so much."

My dad looked crestfallen. "You're not staying? Cards?"

"Not tonight. I'm tired, and I still have to walk the dog when I get home." Inwardly, I cringed. I couldn't believe how effortless it was to make that up. The truth was I wanted to get back to Elijah's before he went to bed or before my sour sister reemerged from her room, looking for dinner.

Like Clemson, she usually came home from her workout with an enormous appetite, and I didn't want to be anywhere around when her storm made landfall again. Once in one day was enough for me.

I made sure the dark SUV dropped in behind me as I left my neighborhood and made my way back to Malibu. Throughout dinner, I had to measure my words so I wouldn't let anything about Elijah slip, so much so that after only ten minutes or so, I just stopped talking altogether and listened to everyone else.

There was never a shortage of conversation at our family's mealtime, and other than Agatha, I was confident no one even noticed I'd gone quiet. Clemson usually talked enough for the whole table, and because she was still in high school, she had enough entertaining stories to do so.

Elijah had given me a spare opener for his garage and graciously parked one of his permitted vehicles on the street so I could keep my car in the garage. He said he didn't want me having to find street parking every time I left the house and, if it was dark when I returned, said he didn't want me walking alone from wherever I parked to the house. When I asked why one of the bodyguards couldn't walk with me since they were always following me anyway, that just earned me one of his patented head tilts, complete with the sexy hair flop, and I lost all train of thought and whatever point I was trying to make.

Tonight, I just wanted to get inside and get to my room with as little drama as possible. Was that even possible anymore? Seemed like no matter which way I turned, that was what I got. Drama, drama, drama.

While I was unloading the bags I brought from my house, Elijah strode into the garage. This space—while generally reserved for cars that could get as filthy as the roads they traveled or as grimy as the outdoors in general—was as pristine as the inside of the Banks Estate. So, Elijah prowling toward me with bare feet was of no consequence to his usual aversion to tracking dirt inside.

Christ, even his feet were sexy. How was that even possible? I knew if I looked hard enough, this man had to have a flaw. He had to. I was just hard-pressed to find one. Maybe if I didn't get so flustered every time he came within two feet, I could really give him a good inspection. But as of now, I was lucky that I remained upright when he got close to me.

Like now. So I tried for humor instead.

"Honey, I'm home," I singsonged and then gulped when he took one more step closer and wrapped his long fingers over mine that were clutching the handles of the duffel bag I'd just pulled from the trunk. My neck was cranked as far back as it could naturally tilt so I could stare into his fantastic hazel eyes. Eyes that smoldered with an unspoken emotion I really wanted him to elaborate on.

"I missed you, beautiful. How was your visit with your family?" he asked in a sultry voice that made me want to talk about anything and everything except my family. And could we do it without our clothes on, please?

Just thinking about my time there burst my lust haze, though, and I wrinkled my nose. Shocking me completely, Elijah bent forward and kissed the tip of my nose and then stood tall again.

"That good, huh?"

"You didn't have to come out and carry my bags for me. I could've made a couple of trips," I said instead of rehashing what happened with Sheppard.

"I don't mind helping you, Hannah. Nice subject change, though. It gives me pleasure to do things for you. It's frustrating that in the spirit of independence, you lose sight of me showing common courtesy. My parents weren't in my life long as far as years, but while she was around, my mother left a good impression."

The look on my handsome keeper's face was so incongruous with speaking of one's parents.

"But not your father?" I asked, hoping he'd share more with me. Up to this moment, he'd not told me a single thing about his past. Especially not his childhood or family. I didn't even know if he had siblings.

"Do you have plans this weekend?" Elijah asked, abruptly changing the subject.

I narrowed my eyes at him skeptically while he prattled on.

"I was thinking maybe we could do something. Be seen in public, you know? If these assholes are still following you, it might lure them out a bit. Being out in public gives both the hunter and the hunted a false sense of security."

"Way to change the subject, Banks," I said, using his

words from a few minutes before. "But it's funny you should ask about my plans, because I was going to ask you on a date, of sorts."

A delicious grin spread across his full lips. Just like that, I wanted to nibble on every inch of him, starting right there with that sensual, mesmerizing mouth.

"Oh yeah?"

I swallowed hard—twice. "Yeah," I finally said when I thought it was safe to speak without my voice betraying the lust coursing through my body. "I have a hobby I don't think you know about, but I thought it might be fun to share it with you."

"Oh yeah?" he asked again, his hazel eyes lighting from the inside like a little boy on Christmas morning. "Is it Shibari?"

"Shibari? I don't know what that is," I said hesitantly. Based on how excited he was, there was no way he could be so enthusiastic about something I loved too.

Then came the devilish grin I recognized. By the time he tightly gripped my hand in his and started tugging me inside the house, I knew I was in big trouble.

Even before he turned to look at me over his shoulder and said, "Come on. I'll show you."

CHAPTER SEVEN

ELIJAH

My God. If I thought her confidence was like doing shots of a potent aphrodisiac, her trepidation was like mainlining the stuff. Hannah tried to tug her surprisingly strong hand from mine, but I wouldn't surrender a millimeter of my hold.

"Elijah. Wait. What are you going to do?" She darted her gaze around the cavernous great room. The light spilling into the space from the kitchen was just enough to allow me to keep tabs on her expression.

"Elijah!"

My next action happened in one fluid motion so she couldn't protest. Hearing the panicky edge in her voice sharpen to a dangerous point told me what to expect when I spun to face her. My senses didn't fail me—it was a rare occurrence when they did. All in one move, I pivoted to face her, dropped her hand from my grasp, stepped right into her personal space she normally guarded like a Rottweiler, and folded her into my body with my long arms.

"I was teasing you, beautiful." I pressed my lips to the side of her head and just stood there, breathing her in. She was intoxicating and invigorating in the same breath. The clean, almond scent of her expensive salon shampoo mixed with her body's perfect natural essence. The resulting combination was dizzying, and I filled my nose with one hit after another. With our height difference, I could enjoy her bouquet, and no one was the wiser. But in fairness to the trembling woman in my clutches, I had to remind myself why I was being allowed to hold her so freely and so . . . oh, yeah . . .

Because I'm an asshole!

Hannah's heart jackhammered in her chest, and I could feel its wild cadence where her body pressed against mine. The problem, however, was her erratic pulse wasn't from lust or excitement like I'd fantasized about in that quick minute before the intended fun turned into a shit show.

But this didn't add up. The stunning, normally independent and feisty woman in my arms was trembling like she was terrified. Even if she didn't know what I was talking about with the Shibari comment, should that really have sent her into a spiral like the one she was trying to recover from?

She was still panting in rapid, shallow breaths. In the glowing light from the adjacent kitchen, I could see the fine sheen of perspiration on her flawless skin. I ushered her over to the tufted velvet sofa and nudged her to sit. I flipped on the antique brass lamp on the end table so the corner of the room was bathed in a warm amber glow.

Hannah hadn't moved from where I'd pushed her to sit on the cushion. She hadn't relaxed into the softness of the sofa's high back, nor had she scooted to the end to nestle into the coveted corner spot against the high back on one side and the arm rest on the other. Instead, she was sitting there as though she were waiting her turn outside the principal's office and her chair was covered with fire ants.

I took the corner spot and spoke quietly. "Hannah, can I hold you? Please. Let me comfort you."

There wasn't a scenario that made me more uncomfortable than causing distress or discomfort to a woman—unless that was expressly the goal of our joining. I needed to fix this. So often, I'd seen my mother suffer at the hands of that monster she married—my father—that it became one of my own scars that I avoided examining at any extent necessary. I was sure my therapist would be so proud that I was connecting this current situation with Hannah and the overwhelming repairman compulsion I was feeling. *And look at me!* I drew the parallel all on my own! It only took seven years of therapy to get here.

"Beautiful girl," I crooned and stroked hair away from her face. A fine sheen of sweat dampened her curtain of blond hair and glued it to her forehead. The effect was probably something she appreciated at the moment because she could hide in the depths, but I wasn't having any of that plan. But when I took a second pass at her hair to clear it from her face, she recoiled as if I burned her.

"Hannah," I said quietly but firmly, "I was just playing around. What is this all about? Help me understand so this doesn't happen again."

"Just...minute," she breathed harshly through the two words, making me think others had been lost in her exhalations.

I'd seen enough people suffer through anxiety attacks in my life to recognize the signs. I sat back a few inches and let fresh air envelop her. I tried to give her the space she needed, but it was taking every bit of effort I could dredge up.

"Tell me how to help, baby. Touch or no?"

Goddammit. Useless was not an outfit that suited me—no matter the season.

"Not...yet...please."

Incrementally, her body began to relax beside mine, and I began to loosen the vise grip I had on my phone, which I had in case I needed to call 9-1-1, but now that I knew she'd be okay, I set it beside me on the sofa. No matter how many times I saw someone go through something like this, it frightened me.

"Can I get you some water, baby?" I asked gently.

"Yes, please," she replied with an overly bright, forced smile.

"Don't do that," I said with a frown, and before she could defend the bullshit, I strode from the room to get her a bottle of water. I was back in moments with two bottles and handed her the one I already opened.

"Thank you."

"For what, exactly? Causing you to have an anxiety attack? Oh yes, you're welcome." I chugged back half the bottle I saved for myself before I could say anything else.

"Elijah, please don't be mad at me. Sometimes this just—"

I scrubbed my open palm down my face but stopped halfway when I realized she was midstride an apology. "I should be apologizing to you, not the other way around. For pushing you in the first place. I'm such a bastard."

Hannah went to say something, but I whirled on her, again not keeping my frustration in check when I saw the phony cheerful mask she slid on.

"Don't."

"Don't what? You didn't even give me a chance to say anything."

"It's this bit you have going." I waved my hand in the air in front of her as though I were casting a magic spell.

"This . . . bit?" she asked with more than a little confusion.

"Like you're about to cartwheel onto a thick blue mat for

a cheerleading competition. Who do you normally have to do this for that it's such a knee-jerk reaction?"

With rapt interest, she studied her water bottle and swallowed so hard I could see her throat bob even in the dimly lit room. But she didn't answer me. Just stared at that damn water bottle.

With my voice in the deepest register I had, I said, "Look at me."

Her blue eyes searched mine cautiously, and I tried to convey one simple message. *You are safe.*

Above all, she needed to believe that. I was a dominant man, true. But I would never hurt a woman. I was nothing like my father. I understood the difference with unerring clarity.

I held her gaze but didn't touch her otherwise. "Now answer me."

"I—" she started and then abruptly stopped. "It's not—" and then stopped again.

Something about her stuttered inhale finally broke through my thick skull. She'd just had an anxiety attack, and I was right back in her face pushing her for answers she didn't want to give me. I should back off and give the girl some space and hope she'd come to me on her own. Just because waiting was so far outside my comfort zone didn't mean it wasn't exactly what she needed.

But that wasn't good enough. If she got away with running when I pressed her for more this time, she'd use the tactic again and again.

"Actually, Elijah, it's been a long day. I'm just going to head to my room if it's all the same. I'm really sorry about this whole..." As she stood, she waved her hand through the air, I guess to symbolize the anxiety attack.

"I'll tell you what, beautiful. Why don't you go ahead and get ready for bed, and I'll be in in a few minutes?"

"Huh? What do you mean?" Her bewildered expression was priceless.

"To tuck you in, of course," I responded, unfazed. Boy, did I call this or what? Definitely wasn't letting her off the hook now.

"Elijah, that is so unnecessary."

"Oh no, it's totally necessary. After this whole"—I made the same ridiculous hand gesture she just had to encompass the anxiety attack—"I don't think I'd sleep tonight not knowing that you got to bed okay. In fact..." I stroked my stubble-roughened chin a few times. "Yeah..." I nodded soundly as though I just made the most important decision of my adult life.

Shit—maybe I have.

"I better just sleep with you tonight. I'll get changed and be in shortly."

I pulled her close to me, kissed her forehead, and then left her standing in the middle of the great room, beautifully bewildered as she tried to come up with something to say in rebuttal.

Turning around, I walked backward down the hall toward my own room. "Don't take too long, and we'll have time for a bedtime story." Intentionally adding my sexiest grin to the mix afterward, I saw Hannah's lips part when she needed more oxygen.

I couldn't help myself. I knew I shouldn't keep fucking with her, but I couldn't bring myself to stop. Maybe if I just got inside her perfect body and slaked the agonizing desire I'd battled all day long while thinking about her, this need to push her for more would stop.

After locking up the house for the night, I went down the hallway that led to Hannah's suite. Light still came from the gap beneath the door, so I tapped lightly a few times on the solid wood frame.

My pretty guest opened the door about five inches but didn't readily stand aside or verbally invite me in.

"We really can say good night here, Mr. Banks. You can see I'm totally fine."

"Nonsense. What kind of host would I be?" My palm met the center of the door, I gave a little push, and she moved out of the way. "I'll even lie on top of the covers if that makes you feel better. And I can go to my room once you're soundly sleeping. I thought I heard you having a nightmare a couple of nights ago." I strode to the center of the room and spun back to face her when I sensed she hadn't followed me. "Do you have those frequently?"

I was shirtless and in a pair of white cotton drawstring pajama pants. My skin had a natural olive hue, so I looked tan year-round. The amount of time I spent outside swimming added to my skin's golden glow. The low light in Hannah's room wasn't hurting the overall effect, either.

When I turned back to face her, she was gawking so hard I had to hold back at least five different comments that would've done nothing but embarrass her and make me sound like a conceited ass. While some might argue that to be true, I didn't have to be the one proving it.

"Beauty?"

"Oh, I think you're the beautiful one in this room, man. My God, you are glorious. I want to take your picture and send it to my sister so she understands what I'm dealing with here."

I waggled my brows so she understood I was being playful. "Do you want me to pose on your bed? Or more of a candid?" If she wanted to snap my picture, I had no problem with it.

Hannah continued to stare, but now it was disbelief in her expression. "You would really go along with that?"

"I think I'd do just about anything you asked me to do, Hannah. But I have to admit, I like that you've been talking to your sister about me." Shit, I thought I might be blushing and was grateful once more for the olive skin tone.

"You don't even know what we were talking about. I could've been saying the most insulting things," she suggested and started taking the decorative pillows off the bed, so I went to the other side to help.

"For one thing, I don't think you're that kind of person. I realize I don't know you very well—or at all, in the grand scheme of things—but it's not the impression I get from what I do know. Secondly, the fact that you talked about me to your sister means I was on your mind, and I like that. Because I think about you all day, too."

After my admission, we both just froze on either side of the bed, each with a pillow in hand. I was cursing the giant mattress between us, but given her skittishness before, Hannah was probably grateful for it.

"Does that bum you out?" she finally asked, breaking the tension that mounted between us like a house of cards. Beautiful and breathtaking but precarious and fragile at the same time.

I tilted my head to the side, hair flopping with the momentum of my body's shift, letting her know I didn't understand the point she was trying to make.

"Well, you said yourself you enjoy punishing women. If

I obey all the rules, you won't have an opportunity to punish any—"

And that was where she stopped talking. Just cut off midsentence and didn't offer an explanation as to why. It had been three years since I'd weathered the Hensley storm, but I swore women were more complicated now than ever.

Isn't navigating through this shit supposed to get easier?

"What? Why did you stop so abruptly?"

"Nothing." She shook her head. "Never mind. This day has already been long enough. I don't need more problems. I just want to get in bed and go to sleep." Hannah dropped her robe, pulled the covers back swiftly, and then raised one knee to the mattress. "You have very nice bedding, by the way."

I was transfixed, watching her climb onto the mattress in a pair of little shorts and matching tank top. I'd seen women dressed in everything from the finest silk and lace lingerie to designer evening gowns, but nothing came close to the vision of Ms. Hannah Farsey in her cotton tank top and booty shorts sleep set.

Fantasies assaulted me as she got comfortable beneath the sheets. I had to close my eyes to stop myself from mounting her and claiming her. It would all happen so fast—she wouldn't have a moment to utter a single word of protest. Mental images of pulling the cotton crotch of those shorts to the side and finding the treasure nestled behind the soft fabric pummeled my brain. When I grazed across her pussy for the first time with the back of my knuckles, I would be able to feel the heat from her core and the wetness of her arousal on my fingers.

"Sweet mother of God," I murmured with no intention of her hearing me. "Do you mind if I get under with you? I can hold you better that way. But if you'd rather I keep the bedding between our bodies, I will respect that."

"So noble, Mr. Banks." I could hear the smile in her voice, but since she already lay with her back to me, I couldn't see her face.

In response, I admitted, "Not always, I'm afraid. But I know you had a long day, and I don't want to make it worse than I already have."

"I think you can be trusted under the covers with me. Just don't make me regret that decision, okay?"

"I'm not a high school boy, Hannah. I can control myself."

I slid between the sheets and arranged the pillows to my liking. Fuck me, this bed already smelled like her, and whatever chance my dick had of not perking up to a full erection was completely lost after I pressed my nose into the pillow a third time. I'd have to be sure to tell the staff to keep the bedding on the bed when she left my home. That way she'd never be too far if I needed to catch a fix. A smell fix, at least.

"Are you a cuddler?" she asked while turning off the lamp by her side of the bed. I heard a shimmer of mischief in her husky voice as darkness settled over the room.

"I suppose in certain circumstances. Like right now, for example. I'd pay money to cuddle with you. To hold your perfectly delicate body against mine. What about you?"

"I'm not really sure, to be honest." She settled onto her back, and it was better to talk this way. Now I could see her expressive face in the filtered moonlight that bathed the room in a bluish glow.

"How can you not be sure?" I placed my open palm on her abdomen. "Either you like snuggling or you don't." It seemed pretty simple to me.

"Elijah . . ." She sighed heavily after saying my name.

Christ, why was just saying my name such a weighty, burdensome task for her?

"Yes?" I finally answered.

"I haven't been in many relationships, you know? And the handful of guys I have been involved with . . . well, I didn't move in with them or vice versa. There just weren't a lot of cuddling opportunities."

"You didn't sleep over? They didn't at your place either?" I pressed for more information.

"I live with my parents and four younger sisters, remember? Not exactly conducive to sleepovers with boyfriends." Hannah barked out a laugh. "Ha! Not to mention, I think my dad would literally birth a litter of puppies if one of us brought a guy around for a sleepover."

"Oh, beautiful! You've been missing out on one of the best parts of adulting. I think from this night forward, we have to sleep together." When she raised her eyebrows in skepticism, I cut off any negative thoughts with a bit of levity. "And don't get any funny ideas either, woman," I said with mock sternness, but at least it earned me a hoarse giggle.

Then Hannah offered, "Well, I think we should see how this experimental night goes first and take it from there."

I had to counter with something, if nothing else, just to maintain the upper hand in the conversation. "Best two out of three, then. To make it fair. Think about it. One night either way could just be a fluke. This is all just statistics and probabilities I'm talking about here. Math mixed with science and all. You get that, right?" I looked at her like I was explaining something dire and complex and trying to hold in my laugh the entire time.

"Oh, absolutely. One hundred percent pure science."

"Now back that sweet ass up. I need to feel you against me while I fall asleep. In the name of science."

And my beauty did exactly as I told her.

"Are you getting a boner? Seriously? I've barely made contact with you. Plus, look at me. I look hideous."

"Oh, baby, I've been able to do little else than look at you since you crashed into my world. But don't worry, until you beg for it, my cock is staying safely in my pants."

"What makes you think I'd even want you like that?"

Now she was taunting me. With the firmness of her round ass, she pushed back against my hard shaft while she asked.

Driven by instinct, I brought my hand to her hip to guide the motion, but Hannah stopped moving before we could pick up a rhythm. So many times this woman's actions or comments screamed how inexperienced she was. It was almost cruel to both of us that we'd landed in this situation.

"I think I've heard rumors that you have a different woman in your bed every night of the week. I'm pretty sure I heard you with one or two of them last week when I first got here."

This wasn't the first time a comment like this had come up, so I knew my manwhore ways bothered her. Even though I didn't know her then and I wasn't involved with her, pretend or not.

"No. You most definitely did not," I replied pointedly.

"It's not like it matters. You don't answer to me, Elijah."

"It does matter," I bit with barely bridled frustration. "I'm telling you I haven't fucked anyone or anything other than my hand since you've been in this house."

"What do you mean? A man with a double standard? I don't understand." She forced a chuckle out alongside the stiff shake of her head, and it was the most awkward sound and jerky head gesture combination I'd ever seen executed.

"That should be a damn felony right there," I commented, letting my chin waltz from side to side. Her movements were typically so graceful and enthralling to experience that having to watch her perform something so unnatural as that last combo she tried to pull off . . . well, it was downright painful.

"A felony?" Hannah questioned. "Like murder?" The sexy little smirk that spread across her lips when she thought she was being clever made me want to sink my teeth into her. Somewhere . . . anywhere . . . everywhere.

I pointed at her and said with excitement, "Exactly! You're killing me, girl."

"Really? What's my weapon of choice?" She rolled her beautiful blue eyes heavenward and mumbled beneath her breath, "I seriously can't wait to hear this."

"Watch it now. Don't misunderstand my playfulness for tolerance. I know you have better manners than that. Rudeness is right up there with dishonesty."

"Were your parents very strict when you were a boy?"

"No, they were dead. For the most part, anyway."

Hannah turned toward the middle of the bed to face me. "I'm so sorry. I didn't know. I shouldn't have . . ."

"Don't stress about it. I was young. I don't have a lot of memories of either one of them. The ones I do have aren't pleasant, so don't feel bad."

"Why? What happened? Oh, you know what? I'm being so forward and rude. Forgive me, please. I think lying in this intimate position is giving me a false sense of closeness, and I'm completely forgetting my place. I hope you can forgive me."

Changing the subject seemed like the best way to derail her self-flagellation.

"Don't be so hard on yourself. It's really not a big deal. Now tell me what happened at your parents' house tonight. You weren't in the best mood when you came home, and then when I teased you about Shibari, you had an anxiety attack over something pretty innocent. Makes me think you were already on edge."

She chewed on her bottom lip a little but didn't answer. I couldn't tell if she was considering what the best way was to explain the situation or if she was trying to come up with another diversion.

"Do you want me to give you a choice? Will that make it easier for you to talk about it?"

"That's a good tactic. It just might work. It will take the burden off my shoulders, and I've been realizing that I really need more of that in my life. But I also know I'm the one that has to relieve myself of a lot of them."

"You're right, you have to do the leg work, no doubt about it. But I might be able to help steer you in the direction you want to go. Especially if we talk more openly about things going on around us. It will teach me a lot about your tendencies."

"I'm not going to lie, man. When you get all bossy and nerdy at the same time? It's ridiculous."

"Is that right?" My eyes were riveted to hers as we flirted. In my thoughts, I begged her to close the gap between us. I didn't think I could continue being noble around this siren for much longer. I wanted her. But the want was speeding way past harmless whimsy, and I needed to pump the brakes or I'd spook her.

After letting a few moments pass by in silence, I reached up and gathered her hair in my hand. "This has to get so hot when you're cooking. I'm surprised you never cut it."

"Oh, I've been tempted, trust me." She sighed with contentment.

"Hmmm. That sounds like there's a *but* in there."

"The man misses nothing, ladies and gentlemen. Stunning good looks and omniscient. You're a dangerous combination, Elijah Banks." Hannah chuckled while issuing the comment, but her mirth was surface level. It was her definite tell.

I'd keep that card close to the vest, though. So far that was all I had up my sleeve. Once I figured out how to play her, all bets were off.

"You don't know the half of it. And stop changing the subject. You think you're clever about it, but you're kind of shit, actually. Whoever you've had to be sneaky around is either dumb or lazy."

She raised one brow and said, "Neither, actually. And maybe you don't know what you're talking about."

"Hmm, interesting the way your first reaction was to defend the person. So, you know you're doing it, but you don't stand up for yourself and change your circumstances. My guess is it's your parents or grandparents, then. This behavior is out of loyalty and respect with a little side dish of guilt thrown in because what else are families for? Now, do I know what I'm talking about?"

"Do you make this stuff up as you go? Just keep taking random stabs in the dark until something sticks? Until you get a rise out of the person you happen to be harassing at the time?"

Given how fired up she was getting, I knew I was really close to the truth if I hadn't hit it on the head squarely.

"I don't do anything randomly, beautiful. Remember that."

CHAPTER EIGHT

HANNAH

Even though I had mentally planned to talk to Elijah more in depth about my past after another week, I wasn't sure a more perfect setup would ever come along like this again. He was being fairly receptive at the moment, and I knew he wouldn't be judgmental. I suspected I'd get the same sort of lecture I always got from my parents: It wasn't my fault. I was a little girl. Things like that.

Well, I might have only been five years old when my view of the world changed forever, but I was old enough to pick up my first burden of guilt that I'd carry—and add to—for the rest of my life.

"I can't believe I'm going to tell you this story." I sucked a deep breath in through my nose. "I haven't told this to anyone other than my therapist. Ever. Jesus, I hope this doesn't set me back. Maybe I should just not."

I looked up and found his beautiful eyes focused directly on me. Only me. I had his complete attention, and it felt like I was bathing in golden sunlight that was warm and inviting… and safe. The overall feeling I always got when I looked at Elijah Banks was safety. He had no idea what that did for my mind, body, and soul.

"Listen to me," Elijah said, brushing some wayward

strands of hair away from my face and tucking them behind my ear. "Firstly, go at your own pace. If you feel like sharing something with me tonight, I'm here to listen. If you decide you aren't ready, I will still be here on the night you are. Okay? Is that a fair plan?"

"Yes. Thank you for understanding."

"Secondly, I realize you don't know me from Adam. I'm pushing you because I'm a pushy asshole. It's the kind of guy I am, and I like you. A lot. I'd like to get to know you better, so I want to know more about you. But I do realize I'm being pushy. Again, you set the pace. But you have to speak up."

"If you had your way completely, what is your pace when you're into a woman?" I asked.

Something about Elijah's laugh before he answered was unsettling. "Let's just say it's been a really long time since I've wanted to know a woman as something more than just a hookup."

He just stared at me after baldly admitting that truth, and I was starting to recognize a pattern in his behavior. He knew it was easier to throw people off a conversational trail by making them uncomfortable with one carefully placed comment or fact than it was to have the conversation at all. It was brilliant, really, because it was highly effective. My natural instinct was to change the subject to something altogether different, and as soon as possible, because my gut was telling me this one was very uncomfortable.

So I had to not let him steer the conversation with this particular trick.

"But you just said you wanted to get to know me better."

"I do. I'm really hoping to break my streak." He grinned.

Based on his expression, he was being playful. So which

did I believe? His words or his demeanor? I couldn't shake the memory of that redhead coming into and leaving his house the first week I was here. Then there had been the comments from Rio about his hedonistic ways. While I didn't expect a grown man to be celibate, I did expect him to be monogamous while in a relationship with me.

Whoa. Back up the wagon, sister.

Why would I even be allowing words like *relationship* and *Elijah Banks* in the same thought?

"Do you have siblings, Elijah?"

"No. Not that I know of."

"You don't think you would know?"

"My father wasn't a good man. I wouldn't be surprised to find out he made bastard children in addition to all his other transgressions," Elijah explained with bitterness in his tone.

"Oh." I really couldn't think of anything to add to that comment. "I'm sorry I brought up an unpleasant topic. I didn't know—"

"Of course you didn't know. You don't have to apologize. It's similar to earlier when you had the anxiety attack that was triggered by something I said. I didn't know it was an issue for you and certainly didn't do that on purpose. Yes, I still felt bad that you were in distress, but I know I didn't personally cause it."

"Have you ever had someone take advantage of that, though?"

"Explain what you mean. I think I know where you're coming from, but I want to be completely sure before answering."

It took some time to come up with a scenario that exemplified what I meant. Finally, I remembered a story that would do the trick. I gave Elijah a sideways glance, trying to decide if telling him this would make me look weak or not. It had always been one of my biggest fears.

"When I was in junior high, I had a friend who knew a little bit about my anxiety disorder. We had been friends for a few years, and inevitably, if I'm around a person that long, they will witness an episode." I waited for Elijah to comment or give some sort of acknowledgment that he was with me so far.

"How old were you when you started having anxiety attacks? Isn't junior high a little young?" he asked with genuine interest.

"I was six. I think in children, the average age of diagnosis is between four and eight."

"Wow, that's incredible. And so sad. I'm sorry you've been dealing with this for so long. It just doesn't seem fair."

I reached out and put my palm on his cheek.

He let his eyes drift closed and just seemed to enjoy the personal contact.

"You're a good man, Elijah. You're thoughtful and kind and compassionate as well."

He held my hand to his cheek but then turned his face so his lips were touching my palm. Elijah pressed a reverent kiss there, and I was speechless from the tenderness of the gesture.

"I'm really glad you insisted on tucking me in tonight," I admitted.

"It's good for you to remember that I know what's best for you."

"Let's not get carried away now."

"Finish your damn story, woman. Then I'm going to kiss you good night and we're going to sleep."

I yawned so big, my jaw cracked. "Okay," I agreed because

suddenly I was exhausted. But then Elijah's words sank in. "Wait. What?"

"Sleep? Go to sleep? That's what the end goal is here, right?"

I narrowed my stare but couldn't stop the grin that spread across my lips. I really wanted him to kiss me again, and now I had incentive to get through this story quickly.

"So my friend witnessed me have an episode, and for whatever reason, it ruined the plans we had. Like maybe we were going to the mall or something. I don't remember the details, but that doesn't matter. But because I had a meltdown, we couldn't go. Of course, we were both upset, but she was really upset because a boy she liked was supposed to be there. I felt terrible about the whole thing, and I kept apologizing and apologizing, and eventually she figured out that I was so guilt stricken that she could use it to her advantage. She asked me for things I had that she didn't—clothes, makeup, jewelry... you name it. She would drop these subtle reminders about me ruining our plans and how she was so embarrassed in front of this guy. She even started making veiled threats that she was going to tell other classmates there was something wrong with me.

"Eventually the stress of being around her became so overwhelming that I broke down and told my parents what was going on. It's such a difficult time being a teen, you know? Well, for me it was. But she was a large part of the problem."

"What did your parents do to help you?"

"As luck would have it, my dad was offered a job closer to where we live now. They were trying to come up with a way to break the news to us about having to change schools, but I was ready to go right then and there. Agatha, my sister closest in age to me, was a little upset, but she got over it. She makes friends very easily, so it was probably more about the change in general.

"And oh my God, I just talked for ten minutes straight without giving you a chance to barely say anything. And it wasn't even a good story. Sorry." I tried my best puppy dog eyes and hoped for good results. I reminded myself he was the one who wanted to hear all of this.

"Do you think people still take advantage of you at this point in your life?"

Well, shit. Why did I feel like I was at my therapist's office suddenly? I wasn't sure I wanted to look at this topic too deeply right now. Or maybe ever.

It took a few hard swallows before words came out when I tried to answer him. "I know what my fatal flaw is, as people say. It feeds a handful of subsequent issues I try to work on. I think acknowledging they exist and trying to have healthy, positive ways to deal with challenges in life is the best any of us can do."

I felt like that was a solid answer, but when I looked at Elijah for his praise and agreement, his face was screwed up in . . . what? Disgust? Disappointment? I didn't know him well enough to understand all his expressions just yet.

"What?" I said with a bit more bite than I intended.

The man slid that tempting smile on and said, "I'm trying to figure you out, Ms. Hannah Farsey, and it's not easy."

I let my head flop to one side like he always did. Somehow, I knew it didn't have the same effect. "What do you mean?"

"This has happened more than once, and I can't figure out why you do it. I think it's an involuntary self-preservation mechanism. If there is such a thing. We were having a great, honest conversation, and then something clicks in your brain or wherever and you slide this everything-is-perfect cheer camp mask on."

I quietly nodded because I knew what he was talking about, and I knew the habit had been exacerbated since I was here.

"So you know you do it," Elijah stated more than asked. "What's that all about?"

"I think it's me not wanting to be a burden to anyone. I don't want to cause trouble or have anyone worry because of something I did or am involved with."

"You do realize that you can't control that, right? If someone cares about you, they're going to worry about you whether you try to guard them from doing so or not. That's not something you actually get a say in."

"But I can shield a person from knowing details of a circumstance, for example, that would compound that worry, don't you think?"

"Maybe in theory," he answered slowly, seeming to be thinking about what I just proposed.

"But . . ." I supplied because I could feel there was more to his stance on this.

A deep wrinkled vee formed between Elijah's eyes while he contemplated his next comment. "Withholding information about something is lying by omission, is it not? And you already know my opinion on lying."

"Yes, but only if you withhold information for nefarious reasons. I'll give you an actual example from my life. My dad has had several heart attacks. His doctors have said his heart condition is directly related to stress and that he should avoid it as much as possible. There have been instances when I don't tell him the whole story because I know it will stress him out."

Elijah stared at me for a minute or two, and I started to squirm under his attention.

Did I just change his opinion of me for the worse? The better? I was really out of my league with this man to begin with, without adding in the fact that I rarely dated. Between my career and family, I'd never really carved out time to get to know someone on the level being in a relationship required.

Somehow, within two weeks, Elijah was extracting information I'd never shared with a boyfriend—or any friend, for that matter. His style of just digging in and not shying away from the hard stuff was an approach I could appreciate.

Finally, he spoke. "I've really been enjoying getting to know you, Hannah. You're smart, beautiful, and interesting." He ran his fingers through my hair from the crown down to the ends, and it was hypnotizing.

"Oh my God, that feels so good. I've said it before, but it's worth repeating." I sighed and sank deeper into the pillow, with a sated smile on my lips. "You're a lethal combination of a man."

Elijah quietly chuckled and then added, "And I told you, you don't know the half of it, beautiful."

After my eyes drifted closed, I said, "I'm not touching that with a ten-foot pole."

"I think you're ready for bed, young lady. Do you want me to stay or go back to my room?" my gorgeous sandman asked.

"Mmm, can you stay until I fall asleep?" I hoped I wasn't asking too much, but he was the one who'd made the offer. At that point it would've been rude to turn him down. Right?

"Of course I can. Are you okay if I keep touching you while you fall asleep? I promise to stay on the outside of your clothes. But lying with you like this is torture if I can't touch you."

"I would like that, Elijah."

"In that case, sleep well, my beautiful girl. I hope you have the best dreams," he offered and leaned in closer to me.

My heart stuttered before it began to gallop wildly in my chest. This was finally it. The kiss I'd been waiting for.

But he kissed my forehead in some unsatisfying paternal gesture instead. My entire body sagged with the disappointment.

"What do you need, baby? Are you cold?" the bastard asked. He knew exactly what I needed, and for some reason, he wasn't giving it to me. Earlier, he was the one who brought it up! I never would have thought about kissing him had he not mentioned it.

Well, maybe never is a strong word here.

"No. It's nothing. I was just relaxing. Good night. Thank you for everything today."

"It was my pleasure."

CHAPTER NINE

ELIJAH

"It's called priapism," Grant informed me with an unsettling air of authority given the topic of discussion.

"Do I even want to know why that just rolled off your tongue so easily?" I looked to my best friend with trepidation.

We walked into Sebastian's office side by side, and Grant wrapped up our conversation with one last comment. "Are you forgetting who followed a married woman around like a love-sick puppy for . . . shit . . . I don't even remember how long?"

I held my hand up to stop him from elaborating. "Enough said, man."

Shark wrapped up his phone call and pointed toward the ceiling. Grant and I fell in step with him, and the three of us walked down the hall to the elevator that carried us up to the roof. This had become our new safe meeting place since the incident at the Abstract kitchen.

Somehow, video footage was taken of Hannah inside the walk-in cooler and immediately sent to her cell phone. The end of the video had still shots of Grant while he was held captive spliced into the feed. When we swept the kitchen for surveillance equipment, we couldn't find a single candy sprinkle out of place.

"Whooaa, dude, look at this! When did you do this?" Grant

was like a kid on Christmas morning with the exuberance in his voice and delight on his face.

"Bas, you really outdid yourself here. Or did Abbi pull this together?" I asked, appreciating the new patio furniture, pergola, and outdoor dining set that sat in place of the old, dilapidated set that basically fell to pieces the last time we met up here.

Of course, Sebastian had to play it cool. But I caught the little grin that slipped out from behind his carefully controlled veneer.

Putting his stoic mask back in place, he said, "Actually, I enlisted Pia to do the honors. You know that woman never says no to a decorating opportunity. Especially when she has her big brother's credit card funding the project."

And that was when he let his genuine smile and radiant pride show completely. Bas was always the first one to sing the praises of his sister, Cassiopeia. Her accomplishments were as good as his own when it came to prideful displays. So he had the honor of leading us to the seating area to show off our new, unofficial, outdoor meeting space.

"Thanks for doing this, man. That other set had definitely seen better days," I said to Sebastian after we all got comfortable on the sofa and love seat.

When Bas didn't respond, I followed his glare across the seating group to where Grant was getting situated on the cushion of the love seat and looking like he was about to put his feet on the table in front of him.

"Dude—" was all I had a chance to say before Bas's growl reached Grant.

"I swear to all things that are holy, Twombley. If your fucking feet touch that table—"

"Oh, here we go again." Grant threw his hands up in frustration. "Are you fucking kidding me with this shit, Shark? We're out-fucking-doors. Birds and mice are going to shit on this table in the next twenty-four hours, and you're worried about my twelve-hundred-dollar loafers."

"All right, boys, that's enough. Let's get down to business." I pointedly raked my gaze down Grant's long legs to his feet. "I thought those were new. Nice choice, man." I nodded a few times before saying, "I know we all have full schedules, so let's talk while we can."

Grant sat up to his full height and leaned forward to rest his elbows on his knees. "Is there any news from any of our sources on the douchebags who kidnapped me?" My friend shook his head in what seemed like disgust with himself. "Fuck . . . that sounds so ridiculous saying that. I'm fucking six and a half feet tall and weigh two hundred fifty pounds. How the hell do you get kidnapped at that size?"

"Don't take this the wrong way, my brother," I said. "Are you still seeing Dr. Shomberg?"

Grant laughed, but it was a forced sound that pained my heart as much as my ears to hear. "Yeah, man, can't you tell?"

This particular therapist had come highly recommended in dealing with patients with PTSD and abductions. At the time, I thought it was unbelievable that there were that many cases similar in nature to Grant's that a psychologist could narrow the focus of their practice to just that cross section of the population.

"Give it time. Don't forget we're here for you, okay?" I offered, and neither Bas nor I spoke again until Grant acknowledged it.

"I know, I know. And I appreciate it. I'm hoping if we

can just make some headway in finding them, it will help me get over some of this." Grant gripped the back of his neck in frustration.

Surprisingly, Bas asked, "Are you still having the nightmares?" He usually just listened to the conversation and added his opinion or information when directly asked for it. He hadn't admitted it to me, but I had a suspicion he felt somewhat responsible for what had happened to our best friend. We all knew who the real target of this bullshit was.

Him.

"Nah, thank God. It's just been those two. The first one when I attacked Rio, and the other one when I fell out of bed trying to fight off my dream captors. The doctor gave me a prescription sleep aid, but I'm not a fan. I was so groggy in the morning. I just don't want to take it if I don't have to."

"All right," I said, ready to move on to the next topic. "There are some growing concerns with Hannah."

"Banks," Grant said with a mischievous grin playing at his lips, "I already explained to you downstairs. It's a known medical condition—"

"I'm going to throat punch you in fifteen seconds, dipshit."

"Explain," Bas issued in his usual business-first tone.

Grant bulldozed right over me when I began speaking. "See, he has it bad for the—"

I launched my entire body at him. Since he was the only person on the love seat and didn't expect me to come at him in a full body rush, I took him off guard and toppled the furniture backward with both of us still on it. When the back hit the ground, the thud reverberated through Grant first and then me, since that was the order of our body stack.

"You're such a jackass," I said, but I couldn't stop laughing at that point because I could imagine how ridiculous we must have looked to a spectator.

"Will you two idiots get up?" Bas grumbled. "For fuck's sake."

I rolled to the side and stood up, then extended my hand to help Grant up too. We both gave ourselves a once-over for wardrobe damage and brushed off the residual dust before setting the love seat upright.

"If you two dumb shits broke that furniture already, Pia will hunt you down at your homes. I'll make sure of it. I'm not taking the fall for this one too."

"That bullshit in your office was your fault," Grant challenged incredulously. "What do you mean, 'this one too'?"

"Let's get back to the situation with Hannah. I noticed on her call log that she's been getting an average of three or four hang-up calls every day. So far, I haven't been able to get a trace on the number, but my team assures me they're getting closer."

"What do they say when she answers?" Bas asked. "Remember, I was getting odd calls before we put Abbi out in Twenty-Nine Palms."

"Oh, that's right. I forgot about that. And she hasn't told me about the calls herself yet. I'm trying to be patient, but it's wearing very thin. The woman doesn't trust or open up very readily, so it's taking longer than I hoped."

"Wait," Grant chimed in, and I could already tell he was going to say something that was going to make me want to punch him again. "Are you losing your touch, Banks?"

"Shut the fuck up, Twombley. At least I knew not to pick a married one, okay?"

Grant put his hand over his heart. "That was low, man. And you are going to get this same bullshit day after day after day for what the two of you put me through with Rio. This is just the beginning, my friend."

"Oh, joy," I said sarcastically while rolling my eyes. My mind was racing all over the place, which was very unusual for me. Normally I was laser-focused and could jump from one subject to the next while keeping up with Grant's ridiculous banter on the side. But today I couldn't think about anything other than Hannah. Was she safe? Did she stay at the kitchen after I dropped her off there this morning? Did she go out to run errands for Rio?

"Grant?" I asked.

"Yeah, man?"

"Is there any way you can call or text Rio?"

"Sure. What's going on? She doesn't always pick up right away, though. If they're busy getting lunch together or whatever, phones go unanswered until they get a break in the action." He explained it as if we all hadn't been exposed to the food prep industry for the past year.

"I get that," I said.

"What do you need from her? I know the two of you aren't planning a Bunco night."

"Not anytime soon, no." I chuckled at the thought. "Can you ask her if she wouldn't mind keeping Hannah inside the building when she's at work? I feel increasingly nervous about her running errands or doing the lunch deliveries if I can't have a bodyguard on her."

"Sure, I'll let her know your concerns. And I'm sure she'll cooperate because she cares about Hannah very much." Grant thought for a few beats. "Why don't you have a bodyguard assigned to her, though? Wouldn't that make the most sense if you're worried about her safety?"

"Like I was getting around to explaining before, she's very skittish. Especially regarding her family. She protects them like she's the parent, even though both parents are still in the picture and not elderly. She's harboring some guilt from something, but I'm still working through all of that. I'm sure I'll get to the bottom of it, but in the meantime, if I could get some cooperation from everyone else, it would be so much easier. I'd be very grateful."

"You got it, my brother," Grant vowed. "I'll ask Rio when I talk to her."

"I was thinking of trying to flush these bastards out of hiding. Maybe make a public appearance or two over the weekend with Hannah and see if that shakes any trees. I'm thoroughly enjoying the woman under my roof, but I'd rather her be there because she wants to be, not because she's forced to be because of circumstance. It's not a great feeling. It's giving me déjà vu, if I'm being honest."

"What are you talking about?" Sebastian asked.

Grant looked at our buddy with utter confusion. "Dude. He's talking about the same thing he's always talking about. Hensley fucking Pritchett."

"I'm not always talking about her," I defended incredulously.

They both did the head-tilt thing in my direction, wordlessly challenging my claim. "Okay, Banks. If not us, at least be honest with yourself," Grant issued and then sat back deeper into the love seat.

Bas studied me for a few really long moments. Finally, he said, "I get the chick did a number on you, man, but I'm going to do something I don't think I ever thought I'd hear myself do—give you some advice about women."

At once, Grant sat forward again. "Oh shit, this should be good."

"You just be quiet over there."

Seriously, I invited Sebastian's advice. "All right, Shark, I'm listening. Let's hear it."

"Women don't like hearing about your past fucks. Especially set on repeat. They're jealous creatures by nature, even more so than men. As long as you're still mooning over Hensley, you'll never stand a chance with Hannah."

"That is what you're saying, right? That you've got it bad for Hannah?" Grant injected his question into the mix.

I twisted my scowl in Twombley's direction. "I don't have it bad for anyone. Christ, we aren't in high school."

The man beamed triumphantly. "That's a yes, then. I haven't seen you act like this about a woman in a long time. I have to tell you, man, I couldn't be happier. Just don't fuck it up, okay? Drop all the shit about the devil lady. Wipe the slate clean and move the fuck on already."

Bas pinched the bridge of his nose between his thumb and first finger while saying, "As much as I hate saying this, Grant's right. It's time to move on. You're wasting your life remembering glory days that weren't all that glorious."

A lot of what my friends were saying was completely true. But there were things they were completely wrong about too. There really had been great times between that woman and me. They just remembered the bad times. These two men were the best friends I could ever dream of having for how loyal and supportive they had been over the past few years.

"I appreciate the two of you more than words can express." I offered my hand to Grant and pulled him in for a hug. We thumped each other on the back a couple times before parting, and then I turned to Bas.

He raised his hand in the air between us. "Yep, I get the point from here. I'm good."

I just shook my head and grinned wider. The guy would never really change, and I guessed that was the great thing about knowing people so well. The word predictable could easily be traded for familiar, and boring could be interchanged with reliable. Who wouldn't want relationships like that?

"Do you want to do something with us this weekend? Like a triple date? I think something during the day would be better. I'd like to lure these crooks out of hiding, and I'd rather not be helping their cause with the dark of night."

Grant stood up and went to look over the side of the building. "I'm in. I'm sure Rio would love to do something with Hannah. To be sure, though, I'll talk to her tonight and let you know tomorrow. Cool?"

"Yeah, that's great. Bas? What about you and Abbigail?"

"I don't see a problem, but I better make sure before committing. A man only makes that mistake once."

I wasn't completely sure what Sebastian meant by that comment, but I had a feeling Abbigail could be hell on wheels to live with. The man had definitely met his match in that spirited redhead.

Grant brought the subject back to the pirates with his next question. "Has there been any other news of pirate trouble? In that shipping lane or anywhere? With that zone being so active, I would think those bastards would be getting a lot of interference with their mid-ocean cargo offloading."

This was my wheelhouse. "I have a team monitoring domestic and international news outlets, and one of my tech guys set up a web-crawler that searches for keywords pertaining to the topic. We've netted a handful of stories that met the search criteria, but nothing that panned out to be our guys." Both friends looked thoughtful while I continued. "After that first story hit the mainstream news, they've either been keeping their noses very clean or are flying so below the radar they aren't being detected."

"Or they've gotten money into the right hands," Sebastian added as a third possibility.

"Good point, Bas," I said. "I hadn't given that much thought."

He shrugged. "That's what I would do. It's the easiest way to accomplish almost everything."

We all nodded thoughtfully, but Sebastian was growing increasingly restless. Grant caught my attention as Bas paced his third lap around the seating area.

"Shark, what is it, brother?" I asked with genuine concern in my tone. If I knew the man at all, his first inclination would be to deny anything was wrong at all.

"Hmmm?" He looked up from where he was inspecting the rooftop. "Nothing. Just a lot on my mind. What else is new, right?"

"Bullshit," Grant disguised in a sneeze and intentionally did a terrible job at it.

"Talk to us," I insisted and held my arm out in invitation for him to join Grant and me.

Bas sat on the arm of the sofa instead of relaxing on the seat. He was as edgy as an expectant father in the hospital waiting room.

"You know, I've gone over this conversation about five different ways, and I can't come up with a single outcome that isn't shitty."

Grant and I both sat forward in our seats too, ready to rally around our friend. That was what we did for each other. We rose, we rallied, we conquered, we celebrated. That was what we'd always done.

"What's going on, man? Just tell us. We'll figure it out."

"Just like we always do."

Bas turned and looked directly at Grant, and I swore I could feel his pain in my own chest when he inhaled to speak.

"My attorneys want to offer Rio a settlement for Sean's death."

"Fuck. Me," I muttered beneath my breath.

"What did you tell them?" Grant croaked after a few long minutes. Then he asked, "How do you assign a dollar value to someone's life? Think about it. Could you put a price tag on Abbi's?"

The look Grant gave Bas was filled with so much anguish, I wanted to blink and, like a whiteboard, erase it from my memory. I never wanted to see pain like that on the face of someone I cared about. Ever again.

Grant cradled his face in his large palms for a minute. When he looked up, he said, "She's been doing so good. This is going to fuck her up all over again. Every time she breaks, I'm scared to death I won't be able to put her back together again. She doesn't deserve to have to keep breaking."

"Now, hear me out, Grant." I raised both hands in front me, palms flat in an *I-come-in-peace* gesture and worded my thought carefully. "Is there any way Rio would take the money and possibly use it to start a memorial fund in Sean's name? Or use it for Abstract? Do something positive in Sean's honor. Taking a settlement doesn't mean she has to buy a Ferrari with the money."

"Or ten," Bas commented, and I quickly shot him a dirty look.

Why didn't the guy just know when to keep his damn mouth shut? I had just made a really good suggestion—a noble idea that seemed like something Rio Gibson could get on board with—and he had to suck the purity out of the moment with a comment like that.

"What?" Sebastian asked incredulously. "It's a very large settlement they're offering. Because it's a combined offer from my workers'-comp policy, the equipment rental's liability insurance, and my jobsite general liability insurance policy, the final total is substantial. These rare occasions are why I pay the premiums I do. If Rio did take the settlement, it would be satisfying to see the money go to someone who would use it for a good purpose."

"I think you should be the one to make the offer to Rio," Grant said after a long moment of silence. "I don't want to be put in the middle of the two of you again, and I want her to hear words like you just said right there"—he stabbed his long index finger toward the ground in front of Bas—"come out of your mouth. I think it would go far in her healing process to hear you sound like a human being, with an actual beating heart, for once."

"You both know that's not what happens when I get in front of other people, though. I was only able to talk that freely because it's the two of you here. I barely sound that relaxed in front of Abbigail, and I'm going to marry the woman. As long as I don't knock her up again first."

Neither Grant nor I missed the devilish grin on his face then.

"You bastard! Have you really?" I asked.

"No, but I'm giving it my best effort," Bas said with complete seriousness.

"She will cut your pecker off if you do. She'll never get into a wedding dress on that plan."

"I just want to see that uptight family of hers at a wedding where their do-no-wrong little sister walks down the aisle eight months pregnant and our son and daughter are the ring bearer and flower girl." Bas described the imagined scene with a wicked gleam in his eye.

"Now I know hell is about to freeze over," Grant said, laughing. "Because that's something Rio would completely conspire with you on."

"All right, gentlemen, I have to head downstairs and get my day started in truth. Are we done here?"

We walked over to the elevator and reviewed what we agreed on. Bas and Grant were both checking with their ladyloves regarding weekend plans, and I pulled out my phone to text my beautiful chef while the two of them discussed a game plan about talking to Rio about the settlement offer. My plan was to steer as far from that hornet's nest as possible.

Good morning, beauty.
Hope your day is going well so far.

I put my phone in the breast pocket of my sport coat so I would feel the vibration if I received a text back from Hannah—or anyone else, but she was the only one I hoped for. I was nearly to my office when I felt the device rumble against my chest. Instantly I grinned and pulled the phone out, only to have my happiness squashed.

*I'm coming over tonight. I know you
miss me as much as I miss you. We're
too good together, Elijah.*

Goddammit. I should've never brought Shawna to my house that first night. She was a wild fuck, no doubt about it, and I was feeling particularly sorry for myself that night and wasn't thinking clearly after too much tequila.

The things I wanted to do to her were not permitted at LuLu's, so she'd suggested we meet somewhere else, and like a dumb, horny guy, I'd brought her back to my house. Now the woman was acting like a love-sick stalker, and if she didn't heed my warning, I'd be calling my attorney about filing a restraining order.

I'm not in town. Call you when I return.

Carmen, my assistant, looked up from his monitor when I strode past him. "Good morning, Mr. Banks. How's your day so far, boss?"

"Well, until about three minutes ago, I would've said pretty damn good."

"And now?" the young man prompted.

"Now I'm just pissed," I growled.

"Is there something I can help with?"

"I don't think so. I got myself into this mess. I need to get myself out. Can you please ensure a car is waiting downstairs in ten or fifteen minutes? Let me know when it's here."

"You got it."

When I got behind my closed office door, I pulled out my phone to see if Hannah had responded, only to find another message from Shawna.

Perfect. That gives me some alone time
with your new friend. Don't hurry home.

Deciding not to message Shawna back, I dialed Grant directly from my desk to his. Hopefully he was already seated by his phone.

"Damn, you're kind of clingy today, even for you. What's going on, pretty boy?" Twombley laughed into the receiver.

"Dude. Fucking Shawna has lost her damn mind," I growled.

My friend groaned on the other end of the call. "Shit. Do I want to know?"

"Probably not, but I need to talk to someone about this or I'm going to storm out of here and go hurt that woman. And probably not in the way she had in mind. How didn't we see these tendencies in her before?"

"Hey, speak for yourself, dude. But again, what did she do?" Grant asked a little more impatiently.

"I got a text from her saying she was coming over tonight. I told her no, that I wasn't in town, and her follow-up text was something like 'oh good, that gives me more time with your new friend' or some shit like that."

"Elijah, breathe for a minute, brother. You're not using your head. The women are at the kitchen in Inglewood and will be for a few more hours. Shawna doesn't know where that is, right? She was just trying to get you riled up."

"Fuck me, you're right." I raked my fingers through my already messy hair. "You're totally right. Well, it worked. I can't even think straight."

"Why don't you meet her somewhere public and explain it to her—very rationally, of course."

"Of course," I sarcastically injected into his plan.

"Do you want my help or not? Because I have about twelve other things I need to do right now, but I picked up your phone call, stalker bait."

"Don't even joke about that. Christ, Hannah's already skittish enough."

"Okay, we are definitely revisiting that. I am, after all, the resident expert on skittish females."

"Ahh, let's not and say we did. How's that?" I offered instead.

Grant made a low hum in the back of his throat before saying, "Oh no, we will. Anyway, meet the redhead somewhere public, break it to her gently that her days of riding Thunder Mountain are over, she needs to exit the park in an orderly fashion, and no one will get hurt."

I couldn't help but laugh. It started as a chuckle and worked up to a full belly laugh until I could barely catch my breath. "Jesus Christ, man. What makes you say the shit you say?" But thank God he did blurt the stuff he did because sometimes a guy just needed to laugh at the ridiculousness of his own existence.

"So what has Hannah so skittish? Is it what happened at the kitchen? Or something other than that?"

"Well, that definitely messed with her pretty badly. She's been having nightmares about that afternoon for the past two weeks. Last night, I finally talked my way into her bed, and I think it was the first full night's sleep she's gotten since she came to stay with me."

"Hold up," Grant said, and I could hear the shift in his temperament.

"Oh, here we go," I muttered. "Are you going to be an asshole now?"

"Can this really be happening? The once famous Elijah Banks, manwhore of all manwhores, is losing his touch. Oh, pretty boy, say it isn't so."

"No, I'm not. Not at all. I happen to have more respect for the woman than a quick fuck. Is that so hard to understand?"

"No, I understand the concept completely." Grant chuckled. "I just thought you no longer did. It's been a whole lot of time, my brother, and a whole lot of random pussy between you and the last time you talked about respecting a woman."

Honestly, he wasn't wrong.

Something had been prickling at the back of my neck since I received Shawna's texts. It took me until now, though, to realize what it was.

"Dude—" I started to say in a rush but completely forgot I was using the phone on my desk. I stood abruptly and pulled the entire phone base with me. "Oh, shit!" I yelped as my cold morning coffee began to topple before I caught the cup and steadied the thing, narrowly avoiding an epic desktop disaster.

"You good, man?" Grant asked.

"Yeah, yeah. Almost had a huge coffee mess on my hands. Anyway, I've had a weird feeling about this whole Shawna thing, outside the obvious weird feelings. You know, something just didn't seem to be adding up, and it finally hit me. Why does Shawna even know about Hannah? I mean, she shouldn't. I made a great effort to keep them apart the one night they were at the house at the same time. And despite what Hannah still believes, it was just one night—the first or second night she was there."

"Why the hell did you do that? Have her over when

Hannah was there? You know how loud Shawna is. If she had even an inkling that someone else was in the house, I wouldn't put it past her to turn on the theatrics," Grant pointed out, only confirming my same thoughts.

"Oh no, man, I didn't invite her over. She just fucking showed up. I couldn't tell you the last time I actually asked her to come over."

"Banks..." My friend just stopped there, and the silence ballooned between us. When I realized how foolish I likely looked through his eyes, I didn't like it one bit.

Lashing out at him seemed like the best option. "You could've fucking said something before this moment, you know? How about that?"

"We both know this isn't my fault and you're just swinging at me because that's the way you deal with shit that makes you look bad."

"Because I've had a stalker how many times before?"

"I've told you that dick was going to get you in trouble, chief. Makes the ladies cray. Zee."

"You're the one who's crazy. And I love you for it, man. Thanks for listening, but holy shit, I'm never going to make it to the Edge on time for this meeting."

"Go. Keep me posted," my best friend said as a farewell.

"Will do. Bye."

Christ. I hated being late for anything. It was a major pet peeve of mine. Well, one of them. As I hustled past my assistant's desk, I said much more tersely than I cared to, "Walk with me." Then quickly added, "Please."

"What's up, boss?" Carmen asked, smart pad already in hand to take notes.

"Can you either call or email Louise Chancellor? Her

information is in my contacts. Please find out the soonest she can meet with me regarding a personal legal matter that involves one of her employees."

"You got it. Anything else?"

"Yes. Can you send Hannah Farsey . . . Do you need me to spell the last name?"

"She's the caterer?"

"Yes. Good memory. Send her flowers from that shop next to the Chinese food place I like a few blocks from here. You know the one?"

"Sure do."

"Excellent. Pick something nice. More than friendly but not red roses, you know? Oh, and not carnations. Make sense?"

"You got it. But just curious, what's wrong with carnations?"

The elevator doors closed on my arm for the second time, so I gave my assistant one last set of instructions.

"I want the card to say, 'Looking forward to our date this weekend.' And I just don't like them. They remind me of senior prom. That night was a clusterfuck I never want to remember again."

He laughed. "I'm on it."

"Thanks, man. You're the best."

"I keep telling you that." He smiled as the elevator doors closed.

I descended to street level and the waiting car that whisked me off to my meeting in the Financial District.

CHAPTER TEN

HANNAH

I was calmer for my final exam at Le Cordon Bleu than I was this morning as I checked my duffel bag for the fifth time.

Elijah was giving his landscaper instructions on some ornamental grass he wanted planted while we were away for the day, but we really needed to get going. The best time to launch was very early in the morning, but the fog was so thick this time of year, very few pilots were brave enough for the Dawn Patrol.

We had plans to meet with Rio, Grant, Abbigail, and Sebastian for dinner at a trendy new place that one of Grant's friends just opened. Apparently, all the men knew the restauranteur since they were all childhood friends from the same neighborhood.

But until then, Elijah still had no idea what I had planned for just us, so he peppered me with questions the entire drive to our destination. Once we got in the general area, though, he got a very sly grin on his gorgeous face and kept bouncing his eyes between the road and where I—also grinning by that point—sat in the passenger seat.

"What do you have up your sleeve, Ms. Farsey? Did you charter a hot-air balloon?"

"Mmmm, not quite. Are you afraid of heights?"

I instructed him where to drive as we entered the restricted area of the field. At the guard gate, I leaned across him, placing my palm on his abdomen for balance, while I handed the security guard my credentials.

"Playing with fire," he groaned when I let my hand linger on his body a moment longer than necessary.

I met his icy green stare. "You don't know the half of it," I teased, thinking specifically of the burner and smaller pilot light that were mounted above the basket.

"I'm going to show you how hot things can get when you hang around me." I followed it with a saucy wink and absolutely no idea where this bravado was coming from.

The guard came back to the car with my license and smiled broadly. "Your crew is on lot five this morning. Have a great flight, Captain."

"Thank you." I smiled back and took my credentials from the man and stowed them in my wallet.

To my handsome date, I said, "Just follow the road signs to spot five." I gestured forward toward the windshield. "They're really well marked here."

Instead of driving, though, Elijah leaned farther into his door and pulled his sunglasses down the bridge of his nose to look at me over the top of them.

"I'm sorry, did he just call you captain? Tell me what's going on, or I'm not driving another inch."

Precisely at that moment, the driver of the car behind us laid on his horn impatiently, and Elijah had to do exactly that. I giggled at his little tantrum being thwarted.

"That didn't work out so well for you, did it?" I taunted.

"Watch yourself, lady."

Chuckling, I deciding to throw him a bone. "Yes, he called

me captain. Do you feel better knowing that? So now you can call me chef or captain. How do you feel about that?"

"I feel like my dick is so hard I'm not going to be able to get out of the car."

When he spoke his next words, his voice was so dark with promise I was grateful I wasn't behind the wheel or we would've been pulling over.

"Tell me what's going on, Hannah."

If I was ever going to keep the upper hand in a conversation with this man, I would have to find a way to strengthen my resolve a bit. As it stood now, with a few spoken words—hell, a single look—I was melting in the seat beside him.

"Hannah?"

I gave my head a little shake. "Hmm?"

"I said tell me what's going on. Jesus, what's gotten into you?"

"Sorry. I'm just excited." I grinned. "I wanted to surprise you today, so I'm glad I pulled it off. I just got my private pilot certificate a couple of weeks ago, so I'm not ready to take friends up with complete confidence yet. The people we are going up with today were all in my class or were my instructors at one point or another. We all do ground crew duties for each other to get more time around the ships and build our confidence with handling the lines and equipment. It's the only way you get proficient, you know?"

I looked over to Elijah, and he was listening with what looked like awe. I felt so embarrassed when I realized I had been going on and on about my hobby.

"I love hearing the passion in your voice right now and seeing the excitement on your face. I'm already grateful you decided to share this with me today."

He held his strong hands out, palms flat and facing up so I could place mine on top. Elijah wrapped his long fingers around mine and brought my knuckles to his full lips for reverent kisses.

I couldn't tear my eyes off him while he tended to me this way. It was a tender side of him I hadn't seen much of.

Through the partially opened car window, I heard one of my former classmates greet me from nearby. Our private moment was over, but our fun day was just getting started.

Elijah turned out to be a great help. He joined in with the rest of the crew and did exactly what the crew chief asked of him. He was extremely fit, and it served the whole team well a few times when the wind gusted unexpectedly before we took flight. His extra muscle and weight were needed to keep things under control.

Once in flight, the experience was even more magical because I got to share it with this man. I was alternately thrilled and scared because I was really becoming interested in him. He told me he had never been in a hot-air balloon before, asked a bunch of typical first flight questions and a lot of unexpected, complicated physics-related questions too.

We landed a few hours later, and I was completely exhilarated and exhausted at the same time.

With Elijah's house in Malibu, dinner would be less than an hour from home in West Hollywood. We decided to go home to shower and change between ballooning and our meal reservations.

But I made the monumental mistake of lying on my bed after taking a nice, hot shower. The next thing I knew, Elijah was kneeling on the floor beside my bed, stroking damp hair away from my face.

"Hey, beautiful. I think you crashed on me." His sultry voice wrapped around me like a velvet cocoon. I might have been dreaming, because the most delicious cologne tickled my nose like I was in the finest spice store in India. No, I had to be somewhere even more exotic, because the most alluring man was smiling down on me when I rolled to my back and gave a lazy stretch.

"My God, what is that smell? I could eat you," I groaned in my half-asleep state and imagined him taking a seat on my bed right alongside my hip. Thinking of his grin tilting one side of his sinful mouth, I squeezed my thighs together in response to the tightness building in my belly.

What the hell was going on? He wasn't touching me. Hell, I was pretty sure I was dreaming, but my body was betraying me in the most carnal way. The only thing I knew for certain was I wanted that mouth on me . . . everywhere. Dinner could go on without us, and Elijah Banks could make a meal out of me instead.

"Hannah?"

"Mmmm." My name sounded so nice through his perfect lips. Everything about him was perfect. I had to be careful not to tell him that though.

"Yes, please. Touch me. Kiss me." Damn. Dream me was bold. Just saying what I wanted like a bossy wench. I could learn a thing or two from this version of me.

"Beautiful, I'd love nothing more, but I think you're still dreaming. And believe me, baby, when I put my hands and mouth on this perfect body, I want you to be wide awake and watching every single thing I do to you. Every kiss I give you."

I could swear I felt his lips brush mine.

"*Mmm* . . . every place I explore with my fingers . . ."

And yes, then his long, knowing fingers danced over my collarbone and across to the other side. Finally, as if all those delicious, torturous touches weren't enough to endure without moaning or gasping or writhing in pleasure, it was his words that made my breath catch somewhere between my lungs and brain. I became so dizzy with lust and need, I was on the verge of begging him to fuck me.

When he was aroused, Elijah's voice was dark and persuasive. There was a seductive, street-worn edginess to it that made my lady parts whimper and want to surrender to his filthy suggestions, no matter what he came up with. The air was charged with sexual tension, and it was a wonder I could hear his declaration over the sound of my own heart throbbing as it pumped more blood to the swollen tissue between my legs.

"I want to see it. No, I need to."

He studied my face, and...I couldn't pretend to be sleeping anymore.

That damn voice. Those seducing eyes. I lay on top of the covers in just a short, white, terry bathrobe and let my eyes slide shut again. It was so much easier when I didn't have to look right at him.

"Open your eyes, Hannah." And now his voice sounded like a spoonful of gravel went down sideways.

"Elijah..."

What was I going to say? Plead for him to touch me? Plead for him to back away? Plead for him to go to his room and get ready so I could do the same? Then we could go sit through an endless meal with our friends and act like none of this happened?

"Let's do this." Every word sounded like a growl now. Low and rough but not cruel or angry. Definitely intense, though.

"I'll give you a choice. Yes?"

"Oh-oh-kay," I agreed. Probably the most foolish thing to do, not knowing what my choices were going to be.

"Show me your pussy. I need to see it right now. It's all I can think about. Are you wearing panties?" He stared at me, completely expecting an answer. If I weren't so turned on, I'd have the good sense to be embarrassed.

All I could do was shake my head. I didn't think I could just bare myself to him like that, though.

So I asked, "What else?"

"What do you mean what else? I'm going to have to go to my room and beat off so I can sit down comfortably at dinner tonight. Even that might not work, because I look at you and all I think are really, really filthy things that I want to do to your body. Things I'm almost positive you haven't done before or even knew were possible."

I swallowed the knot of anxiety that started gathering in my throat because there was no way I was going to let that old hag ruin this moment. No. Way.

"I meant, what is my other option?" I watched with rapt attention as Elijah thrust his hand into the waistband of his track pants and readjusted himself. There was an unmistakable erection pressing at the soft fabric, and it was alarmingly large.

Jesus, Mary, and Joseph.

"I want to kiss you. Freely, properly kiss you."

"Yes." I rushed out the word. "I want that too."

"I want to lie with you while I kiss you."

"Yes," I said again, more eager than I could remember being about anything. But I should've insisted we slow down so I could memorize every single detail of the moment.

First times only happened once, my mom always told

us. Savor the moment. Don't let it rush by without enjoying the whole experience. I knew she was right. After twenty-six years of either hearing her preach the life lesson or hearing her apparition when she wasn't there in truth, I knew I should've slowed down.

But I could not.

I held my open arms out in welcome, and Elijah came to me. My God, this man was beautiful. I really wondered if I was still dreaming, and if I were, I had no interest in waking up.

The mattress dipped toward my handsome housemate as he settled in beside me, and I naturally gathered a little momentum to roll toward him. His devilish smile was replaced by a different one I hadn't seen before. Equally devastating, similarly breath-robbing, but much more genuine than the other versions he'd bestowed upon me thus far.

"You are painfully handsome, Mr. Banks." I smiled and touched his smooth skin. "And you shaved. Normally you have a bit of growth here, but I like the smoothness too. I think you could have blue skin like that movie . . . shoot, what was that called?" I snapped my fingers a couple times, trying to conjure the title out of thin air. "They lived in trees or something?" *Snap, snap.*

"*Avatar*?" he asked with a chuckle.

"Yes!" I snapped my fingers and pointed at him. "That's the one."

Elijah grabbed my hand out of the air between us and brought it to his mouth. Everything else around me—around us—there on that bed fell away. The universe shrank down to a queen-size mattress in Malibu, California.

"Are you too tired to go to dinner?" he asked and sucked on my little finger while I watched. When I didn't answer, he bit down into the pad on my fingertip. It felt good at first, but the pain grew to something I couldn't handle, and I widened my eyes before starting to panic.

He let go seconds before I freaked out. My heart thundered in my chest, and Elijah slid his large hand up my neck until his fingers pressed in on my pulse point there.

"Do you feel that?" he asked, looking into my eyes. His hazel was so much more brown in this light.

"It's hard not to," I croaked. "It's quaking my entire body."

"You're so responsive. It's incredible."

I just smiled—or tried to, anyway. He quirked a brow my way, and I expected as much. It was the exact behavior he had called me on numerous times before, and if it wasn't such a habit, I wouldn't have pulled it again now. Of all times! He and I still needed to have a long talk, and I wasn't sure he was going to like what I had to tell him.

After I spilled my dirty dishwater into his pristine sink, I prayed he wouldn't kick me out of his kitchen. Only time would tell. In the meantime, I did not want to destroy this moment with the bullshit from my past. It had already taken over so much of my life, and I refused to keep getting in my own way.

"Can I touch you?" I asked him, not knowing what he preferred.

"I want you to just enjoy me touching you right now. Fair?"

"Mmmm, I'm not su— Oohhh. Wow, that feels good."

"Turn away from me, beauty. Lie on your side."

"But I thought we were going to—"

His censuring look made me comply. I just didn't know how we could kiss if I wasn't facing him. And I really wanted to kiss him.

Elijah made a big pile with my hair on the pillow above my

head and moved in closer with his muscular body. He started making a trail of wet kisses behind my ear and worked his way down my neck and across my shoulder.

"Lie on your stomach, beauty."

When I willingly complied, I knew the war was over for me. That request, that moment in time. If I thought I was still holding my own in a battle with him, I hoisted my white flag right there and then.

I just wanted to feel good. And my God, did this man know how to make it all feel so damn good. His lips were melting me everywhere they touched. I let him move my body like a puppet—just arrange me to suit his plan. I still lay on my stomach, and Elijah rested my arms beside my body, palms facing the ceiling so he could draw my robe down my body and expose my back completely.

"You are perfection, Hannah. Just look at you," he said with admiration. He kissed every inch of my exposed back, biting and licking and sucking until I was moaning into the bedding.

Elijah covered my body with his, pressing me into the mattress with his weight. He growled into my ear and ground his dick into my ass crack at the same time.

"Can you come for me, beauty? I smell how turned on you are. Touch yourself or let me touch you."

"Elijah," I whimpered.

His words and questions were so dirty they ramped up my heat further and further. I was going to combust any second.

"Yeah, baby?"

"It feels so good. My God."

"What's it going to be? Are you going to show me how you like it? Or do you want me to find out for myself? One of us is rubbing that wet cunt right now, beautiful."

I moaned at his filthy promise just as my robe hit the ground. How that happened, I didn't even know. Nor did I care.

"Spread your legs for me," he demanded, and I followed his instructions without hesitating. I was so aroused, I was beyond shame or embarrassment. I needed satisfaction more than my next breath.

"Now, tell me," he said while cupping my mound with his large hand and pressing the heel against my wet folds.

God, I needed friction, but when I tried to buck my hips, he stilled my movement.

"Tell you what?" I nearly shouted the question, approaching desperate territory.

"Watch yourself, lady."

"Please. Please."

"Tell me two things first."

"I'll do it myself. Move your hand. I'll just do it."

"No. You gave up that option."

I whimpered into the sheets, mumbling, "I hate you, I hate you, I hate you."

The bastard leaned close to my ear and asked, "What happens to liars at my house?"

"Elijah! No! Stop fucking around. You're not being fair. Or nice, at all. What do you want to know? Please don't stop touching me. Please don't stop. I'll be good now."

"I know you will, beautiful."

"Touch me," I whispered, feeling insane with need. It had been so long. So damn long.

"How often do you do this for yourself? Be honest."

"Not very often."

"Not very often ... What does that mean to you? Once a

week? Once a month? Once a quarter? Once a year? Pick one."

I must have waited longer than this cruel man preferred because he barked, "Now!"

"Once a quarter."

"Thank you for being honest, Hannah. Fuck, you're so wet, baby." He had started taking slow front-to-back strokes over my tender folds, and I was thrust right back to the edge of ecstasy. I never pleasured myself with this technique, but I was sure as hell going to be changing that crime against womanhood in the near future.

"Oh my God. Oh my God, why . . ."

"Are you close? Feels good, yeah?"

"So good. I didn't know that. I didn't know." I heard myself babbling but couldn't string a more intelligent thought together to replace the babble.

And then he stopped again.

"No! No. Why are you doing this? Why are you teasing like this? It's so cruel. Just get away. Get off. Get up—" I tried pushing him, but it was no use. I was wrung out from the frustration, and the man had about one hundred pounds of weight on me.

"Stop, Hannah," my sexy man warned, and we both sat up. *Well, he wasn't my man, was he?*

"Is this your idea of fun? Ramp a woman up and then leave her hanging there? Did too many girls bruise your ego when you were a teen or something? I mean, why would you be so cruel like this? What's in—"

I was abruptly silenced when his very demanding mouth pressed to mine. Elijah must've figured it was the best way to quiet me because the other attempts were failures. When I saw he was about to speak, I would immediately launch another verbal torpedo his way. I was fuming when he left me hanging the second time, but now, with his plush lips where I'd wanted them for so long and his skillful tongue stroking mine, I couldn't remember my own name, let alone if I had been mad or happy.

When we finally parted, we were both winded. I gripped his biceps so tightly, my short fingernails dug into his skin and left little semicircle indentations behind. My head spun like I'd just been on an amusement park ride, and I was glad I was sitting on the bed.

The hungry look on Elijah's face was so sexy and dark, I forgot all about being pissed at him and wanted more from wherever that kiss just came from.

I'd suspected this guy was dark, dirty trouble, and I was right. He scrambled my brain and made me irrational by making me focus on feeling things I'd long since stopped feeling. But when he crawled over and straddled my partially exposed body again, I let him push me back down beneath him without resisting.

"Now," he said, holding his body over mine in a plank.

Jesus, I wanted to yank all his clothes off and study his muscles all bunched and flexed from the stress of doing the move.

"Are you listening to me?" he asked, looking like he must have said something else and hadn't gotten a reply in the amount of time he prescribed to be reasonable.

"No. I'm absolutely not. Sorry. Can you repeat the question? And possibly look less sexy while doing so?" I closed the small distance between us and kissed his lips—just a peck this time—and then flopped back down into the pillows.

"You're trouble, Ms. Farsey. I think I better keep a very

close eye on you."

"I'm trouble? Are you kidding me right now?" I squawked incredulously. "Oh my God, this guy."

"Okay, this is the question. Remember, honesty first. Forget embarrassment or whatever."

"I hate these setups you do. I'm just going to tell you that right now. It makes me way more tense than if you just asked the damn question."

He quirked his brow, and I returned the gesture, making him laugh again.

"See? Total and complete trouble."

"The question?"

"When's the last time you were with a man?"

"Oh boy, talk about mood killer." I threw my hands up. "I don't know. I'd say, three years ago." Up with the hands again. "Give or take," I said, starting out with confidence, but because of our proximity, I was able to watch Elijah's expression change as he processed the information. "I'm pretty sure it's like riding a bike, though." But that comment didn't even get a chuckle. "Okay, chief, spit it out. What's the problem? We went from hot sexy fun times to this. I thought your fish friend was the moody one? At least according to Rio, he is."

"Ha, she should talk," Elijah spat with a fair amount of venom.

"Was that in defense of Sebastian or an attack on Rio?"

"Yes," he answered and let a little smile peek out. "You know what? I don't want to talk about either of them. I don't really want to make it to dinner with them, if I'm being honest. I'd much rather stay here and just hang out with you all night. I'm sorry I let all that get to me just then. I get a little sulky sometimes when things don't go my way, or the way I envisioned them going. Only-child syndrome never corrected."

"No way," I said, laying on the sarcasm. "Will you please answer a question of mine?"

"I'll do my best, yes."

"Tell me why my answer changed your mood so drastically. You encourage—wait, no... You insist on complete honesty but then act like a brat when I give it to you. You have a past. I've had three, possibly four, sexual partners in my entire life, and I'm almost thirty."

"Possibly?" He screwed up his face at my weird answer to a very basic question, and I had to laugh at his expression.

"It really depends on who you ask," I said in an effort to clear it up.

"Is your answer three or four?" Elijah asked.

"I say four."

"Why would the other person involved say three?"

"Because he didn't get off."

"Why didn't he?"

"Dude, that's something you'd have to quiz him on. I'd also warn him about your honesty policy beforehand, though. He always struggled with the concept. Not to mention, I'm pretty sure he'd love nothing more than to have his ass spanked by the likes of you. Which may also be the reason he didn't get off with me, if you're picking up what I'm putting down."

Elijah threw his head back and laughed so hard, he had tears rolling down his cheeks. "You're really funny. Has anyone ever told you that?"

"My sister Agatha and I really can get going. I know she appreciates my humor." I smiled warmly thinking of her.

"She's the one you were going to send my picture to."

"That's right. Good memory, Mr. Banks." I smiled at him

because I was probably about to get into trouble. "Not bad for an old man such as yourself."

He narrowed his hazel eyes and stared. I didn't know if he was playing or if he was truly upset. *Uh-oh.* Had I taken our teasing too far?

Before I could defend myself, or protest, or run away screaming to the security guards to protect me, Elijah had me facedown over his knees while he sat on the side of the bed. How he maneuvered us that way so effortlessly and so quickly would probably keep me up at night until I figured it out.

"No! Elijah! Let me go." I was laughing so hard, I could barely hold on to his legs so I didn't topple to the ground. "Move fast for an old man, too."

"Keep going, girl. See what happens."

I wasn't sure who was laughing more, and that gave me an idea. If I fell off him, he wouldn't be able to swat my bottom. Instead of trying to hold on, I started squirming as much as possible so it would be too difficult for Elijah to keep me across his lap. It was a much better plan. I could hear the frustration in his warning tone when he growled my name one last time before my butt hit the ground with a solid thud.

"Shit!" Elijah barked. "Shit, girl. Are you okay? I'm so sorry." Before I could say anything, he scooped me off the floor and stood with me cradled in his arms. We both looked down and realized my robe had fallen off completely.

I was naked in Elijah Banks's arms.

He looked back up into my eyes, and I watched so many different emotions flicker across those icy green irises, it was fascinating.

"What are you thinking right now?" I put my flat palm on his temple and cheek as I had once before, and he tilted his head into my touch. "I know that's completely cliché for a woman to ask a man that, but I saw so many things happen in your eyes in one second. I just need to know. This color of yours shows so many of your feelings." I watched as he digested my words, and still I added, "You are so beautiful."

"Thank you, Hannah."

"You can put me down. I'm not hurt."

"I kind of like this. Holding you here. Especially given your state of undress." He grinned, and I saw a teenaged boy getting away with copping his first feel. Wow ... so many facets to this complex man. I wondered which one was closest to the real Elijah Banks.

CHAPTER ELEVEN

ELIJAH

Dinner was a total bust at that point, and honestly, I couldn't be happier. The last thing I felt like doing was refereeing between Shark and Twombley all night. Throw in the secondhand discomfort of all the women being around each other—yeah, no thanks.

What was even crazier was that shit show was my idea in the first place. The theory was a good one, but when the invitation sprang from my lips, I knew the execution had the potential of being like a reality television show.

Then those crazy texts came from Shawna, and now I just wanted to keep my precious little blond kitten inside the house with me all day, every day, where she was safe and secure and I knew where she was at all times.

Now who was the crazy one?

Another thought crossed my mind this afternoon that could've knocked the air right out of my lungs if I had been in a weaker state of mind when I realized it. But as days go, this one had been epic, so I'd processed the mindfuck and moved on.

Since Hannah had arrived at the house almost two weeks ago, I'd had no desire to go to LuLu's club, or any club, for that matter. Equally, I'd had no craving to use my own playroom at the house. There were so many debauched memories of time spent in there involving other women, and I wasn't interested in any of it.

I was only interested in her.

It felt so good that I couldn't wipe the silly smile off my face.

There had been another time in my life when I'd gotten sloppy like this and let my emotional guard down. I'd believed I could love and be loved and that I deserved to experience the same feelings everyone else around me did. There had been another woman in my life who'd made me feel like I could be a better version of myself—not just for me but for her. That woman had looked at me like I mattered—not for who my parents were or what I stood to inherit but because I mattered. To her, I mattered.

Until I didn't.

I gave my head a little shake because the last thing I wanted was to get morose about the past when the future looked so bright. And the future felt so right as I held this little bundle of hot perfection in my arms and made my way across the house toward my room.

"Where are you taking me, kind sir?"

My cock perked up all over again, and I groaned. "Say that again."

"Where are you—"

I cut her off immediately. "No. Just the last word."

She repeated the sentence to herself, mouthing the words soundlessly until she got to the last one, and then shot her eyes back to mine.

"I thought we were over that."

"Explain."

She groaned. "Oh, not you too. I thought that was Mr. Shark's catch phrase."

I barked out a laugh. "Can you reach the knob?" I asked so she could open the door to my bedroom since my arms were still full of her. "Yes, Bas says that often, but it has rubbed off on Grant and me too. You're very observant, beautiful."

I wanted her beneath me, and I wanted it to happen in my own bed, right the fuck now. I wanted to smell her on my sheets and have her be the first thing I saw when I woke up in the morning. There were so many things I missed about having a legitimate girlfriend in my life and not just a random fuck every night.

I wanted those things with Hannah Farsey.

But I knew it was too soon to pressure her about it.

If she hadn't slept with a man in a few years, there was no way she would be ready to commit to a relationship after a couple of weeks. And really, was I?

But that brought up another question—maybe the bigger question. Why hadn't she been with a man in such a long time? Did I have the right to ask her?

Laughing to myself, I thought, when had that stopped me before?

After laying her down, I stepped back and looked at her, wanting to memorize her there in the center of my big bed. When I closed my eyes, I wanted this to be the first image that came to mind.

My beautiful girl lying there, soaking up my adoration.

Every time I thought it or said it, the claim felt more right. Mine.

I hiked one knee onto the mattress, rested it by her hip, and looked seriously into her ocean-blue eyes.

"What are your thoughts here?" I asked her pointedly.

I wasn't used to having to negotiate how far things were going to go, or not go, in the bedroom. Other than the time with Hensley, I'd spent the better part of a decade doing who and what I wanted . . . and when I wanted to do it. There might be some missteps in my near future as I dipped my toes back into the relationship waters.

Again, only if that was what this queen wanted.

And if I was the one she wanted it with.

"Thoughts regarding what? I mean, be specific, man. I have so many, many thoughts." She had the gall to reach both arms above her head and stretch like the little kitty I kept mentally comparing her to.

I narrowed my eyes in her direction and dropped my voice into the deepest range I could manage. "I want to fuck you, girl."

My cock gave an involuntary lurch in my slacks, and I swore I could feel vital blood nourishing every vessel there. I kept my stare fixed on her, cataloging her reactions as she became aroused again.

Her lips parted, her pupils dilated in the dim light, her gorgeous—and I'm talking fucking phenomenally gorgeous—tits heaved and dipped with each cycle of breath, and her spine arched and stretched in direct relation to her breathing.

When I got to the heaven between her legs, I found my voice again.

"Hannah," I issued from deep in my chest.

"Wha-What?" she panted. She liked knowing I was watching her. Which, in turn, aroused me that much more. I rubbed my dick through the impossibly tight fabric of my pants. The damn things needed to go before I lost blood flow to essential parts.

"Keep still," I said calmly but very seriously.

"What?" she asked while scissoring her thighs.

I slapped her thigh on the fleshiest part in a way that sounded much louder than it stung.

"Elijah! Why did you do that? Shit."

"When we're in this room, beauty, do as you're told the first time. If you can't follow instructions, I can tie you down until you can. Do you understand me?"

"I don't think you had to—"

"Do you understand?" I asked in the same tone.

Unless I was playing with an experienced sub, it normally took two or three times repeating a question before she caught on to her expected response. Hannah and I had already been through these verbal exercises outside the bedroom. She should—and that was a very big should—already be responding properly.

She crossed her arms over her chest and looked at me with an expression I'd seen many times before on different faces. *The internal war.* Argue for the sake of arguing or give me what I was asking for and get what she wanted too. Some came to the decision quicker than others. Some fought until the end of the night when we both collapsed from sheer exhaustion.

I was praying she wasn't going to go down that path.

The fighters were always fun if that was what I was in the mood for, but there was no way Hannah was going to fight. She needed relief too badly. Edging her earlier was a smart call.

"Talk to me, Hannah."

"I understand. But I want to say something else. Is that allowed?"

"Everything's allowed."

"Well, that's not true. Look what just happened when I

rubbed my freakin' legs together."

"After you were told to be still. All you have to do is follow directions, and I promise you will be overwhelmed with pleasure every single time you put yourself in my hands." I stroked some strands of hair back from her face. "How does that sound?"

"And what about you?" she asked.

"What about me?"

"What about your pleasure?"

"Pleasing you pleases me. Hopefully—and I'm pretty good at knowing these things going into this type of exchange—you will find pleasing me pleases you."

Her eyes went from narrowed to a full squint by the time I finished talking. I knew her opinion before she even shared it.

"I'm not submissive, Elijah. I already know that about myself. Maybe I'm the one time you're wrong."

I moved from partially kneeling on the bed to sitting. It was important we talked about this before we ventured any further anyway, so no time like the present. I pulled the throw off the foot of the bed and covered my pretty kitty with it. Covering her body was a crime against mankind, but she'd be bare soon enough if I had my way.

"How's that? I know it can be cool in this room if you aren't"—I rolled my eyes heavenward, trying to be tactful—"being active."

"That's nice, thank you. Everything in your home is so lovely," she commented while admiring the blanket. "Either you have an amazing decorator, or you have exquisite taste in home furnishings on top of all the other things you're amazing at."

"Oh, sweet girl . . ." I grinned, knowing that was the version that got me laid more times than I could count. Then I moved closer to her until our foreheads were touching and said, "You haven't seen anything yet."

"I would really like to, though," she said in her low, sultry voice.

"Yeah, this is going to be good, Hannah. Let's get this talking over with so I can put my mouth to better use."

"Mmmm. Okay." She nodded with jerky movements.

"Enjoying pleasing others, serving others, getting fulfillment by doing things you know will make others happy? Those aren't bad things." I had to touch her while we talked.

Once before, I had explained our connection to her as elemental. My body needed to be touching hers if we were near each other. At least that was how it was for me. I had no idea what was happening to me, but I knew if I didn't find a way to slow down with this woman, I had a big chance of getting hurt again. I felt like I was barreling toward a rock wall and my brakes just went out.

"So, I'm going to go out on a limb because we haven't talked about this yet, but I hope we do at some point. Think about when you cook. What about that experience brings you joy? Why do you do it, and what led you down that path? And if you don't want to talk about it with me here tonight, it may be an eye-opening prompt for self-discovery."

"Someone's been to therapy," she said on a laugh.

"That obvious?" I chuckled too. "Seriously though, what gave it away? I need to cut back on that shit."

"No, don't cut back on anything you do or say. You're amazing. A little intense when a person first meets you, but even that . . . I don't think I'd change."

I shifted my weight on the mattress to loom over her,

bringing us nose to nose. "So you don't find me intense anymore? You've only known me two weeks. I'm doing something wrong if the intensity has already worn off."

She smiled, not catching the clues that this conversation was about to turn a corner and head down a dark dead-end alley where she was going to be trapped between me and a hard place with nowhere to go but down.

Ever so slowly, I stood up, keeping my stare fixed on hers with no discernable expression on my face.

But there was intention all around me. Intention in my inhalations and exhalations. Intention in the way I unbuttoned my shirt and kept her trapped in my gaze, even as I let the thing billow to the ground like a dropped mainsail. And the most assured intention of all as I pulled the end of my belt through the buckle's frame and let the prong pop free of the hole. With a flick of my wrist, the leather *whooshed* through the loops of my slacks and made a small *crack* on the air.

If I hadn't been so raptly fixed in her gaze, I would've missed the way she jumped just a fraction of an inch at the sound. But I was. So I didn't. And even that little action of hers made more blood throb south to my engorged cock. I was never going to fit inside this woman tonight, but damn if I wouldn't get off one way or another. I was in agony from being so aroused, and just the thought of stuffing myself back into my pants without tapping my balls first made me shiver.

Hannah was still using the throw to shield herself from me, so I strolled to the foot of my bed and took the ornamental edge of the coverlet between my fingers and yanked it off her and the bed completely. The blanket joined my clothes somewhere inconsequential.

Next, I set my sights on her sexy ankles. She was a step

ahead, though, because my beauty also had brains, but her plan of scooting her feet out of my reach was foiled by my long arms. I swiped out in front of me and had my prize—one ankle in each hand's grasp.

"Elijah, what are you going to do?" Hannah asked with unmistakable trepidation in her voice.

For some reason, her nervousness excited me. It was rare I had inexperienced subs, let alone lovers, and I kept thinking of more and more things I wanted to do to her and with her. Hannah's lack of bedroom history would make almost every one of them new and exciting. They would all be new and exciting for me, as well.

As I tugged her down the bed, she squealed and then giggled. That adjustment put her flat on her back instead of reclined in the throw pillow pile. It also put her at the end of the bed near some other fun things we could play with—like rig points built into the bedframe that were cleverly hidden in the ornamental styling of the furniture. Beneath those were hidden compartments that housed adult toys and other essential products that were used to enhance the bedroom experience.

I just didn't know how far she wanted to go, and I didn't want to ruin a great day by scaring her. We would have to negotiate the parameters of our playtime as soon as possible. For tonight, though, I just wanted to make her feel good and have her coming back to me for more.

"What do you think's the best part about having sex with someone for the first time?" I asked as I climbed onto the bed and straddled her hips.

She looked up with stress knitting her brows. "Wait."

"What, beauty? You aren't getting a report card here."

With the pad of my thumb, I massaged the crease between her perfectly shaped eyebrows. "I'm just getting to know you better, baby. Relax."

"Oh, good." She smiled and blew out a breath. "I thought if I gave the wrong answer, you'd leave me hanging again. Do you answer too?"

After a simple shrug, I said, "I don't know. If I do, I think you should come up with your own question and not bogart mine." I leaned down and softly kissed her. But instead of kissing her on the lips, I kissed the corner of her mouth where the bow of her soft smile started and stopped. When I drew back, big blue eyes stayed fixed on me to see what I'd do next.

"Come back," she whimpered. "I want a real kiss. One of those toe-curling ones like you gave me earlier. Those kisses you give me that make me all mushy inside."

"You mean that make you wet between your thighs?"

She nodded.

"Ask for it."

She stared at me, and I could only guess she wasn't comfortable talking dirty. We'd rectify that situation, and we would have so much fun doing so.

I reached out to her as I spoke. "I want to devour this mouth," I said and tugged her lower lip between my thumb and index finger. "This pout when you're trying to get your way." I groaned and continued to pull. Mesmerized, I watched a fire build and grow and replace her spirit's normally calm glow.

Hannah lifted her hand to knock my grasp free.

"No." I followed it with, "Down."

Because my beauty was smart and had already picked up on the easy law of this land, she dropped her hand into her lap. Judging by the expression on her face, she didn't appreciate taking orders this way—not one bit. But she still complied.

"God, girl. You are perfect. Now tell me, if I feel your cunt, will it be hot and slick? Or will it still be dry?"

Her throat bobbed with the effort she made to give me an honest answer.

"Are you going to answer me? Or do you want me to just check for myself?"

"Elijah, please," Hannah said breathlessly and scraped her short nails up my thighs.

"What is it, baby? What do you need?"

"Please stop teasing me. I can't take any more," she whimpered.

"I need to taste your pussy. I won't be able to sleep with you under the same roof for another night and not know how you taste between your thighs."

"That sounds like a national emergency, Mr. Banks. The way you're describing it, at least. You're so funny."

"According to my cock, it's a matter of life or death. I can tell you that much." With a lazy grin and flick of my chin in her direction, I asked, "So what's it going to be, beautiful? Are you okay with me spending some time getting to know your cunt up close and personal?"

"Has there been a woman in history who has said no to that?" Hannah chuckled with what I was coming to understand to be a nervous laugh.

"Once I'm done with the first round, I think you'll be begging me for a repeat performance every day for the rest of your life." Kneeling tall, I moved closer and nudged my way between her legs.

Totally shelving the fact that I just thought of all those words in one sentence: the rest of your life.

"Before I rock your world, I want to check out one last detail."

She groaned and thrashed her head from side to side. "Oh my God, Elijah. You're the biggest buzzkill, you know that? Women don't just touch themselves with a piece of cooked spaghetti and get turned on."

"And men do?"

"The point is, you get my motor humming and then shut it off without so much as putting me into park. One more time, and I won't even try."

"My apologies. This is the last false start, I swear. I just felt like it was necessary to say that I don't share. Ever. If you're in my bed, that means you are mine. If you have my dick in you, you have no other dicks in you. Understand?"

"Wow. Born romantic right here, ladies and gentlemen," Hannah mocked. Then, with the focus of a laser beam, she narrowed her blue eyes right at me. "What kind of woman do you think I was raised to be, Elijah?"

The moment I saw the hurt in her eyes, I knew the comment was way over the line. It wasn't the message as much as the delivery. At least, that was what I thought, but shit, I freely admitted this woman confused me.

"Please forgive me," I apologized before leaning in and pressing my lips to hers. I wanted to cover up my idiocy with passion—my ignorance with consideration. "I just—it's just been—fuck, Hannah." Every time I thought I knew what I wanted to say, I'd either change my mind or she would kiss me and I'd completely lose my train of thought.

After. Okay, after I gave her a few epic orgasms, I would apologize again and hope like hell it stuck. I really didn't want to fuck this up with her, and by resorting to my comfort zone of dominance, I might have done just that.

"What's today's date?" I asked Hannah, and her twisted expression was priceless and reasonable for how out of left field the query seemed.

"The date? Jeez, I don't know, I think July fifteenth. Why?" She pushed up on her elbows and watched me.

I wanted to taste every square inch of creamy skin on my way to her glistening center, but my beauty was whimpering with impatience as I traveled downward.

"This is my new birthday. The day I started living again," I told her when I got comfortably in place. "And check it out. My present is right here."

My God, she smelled so pretty and feminine yet earthy and female at the same time. My head swam with dirty thoughts, and my body pulsed with vicious need.

"You're so crazy," Hannah purred, thinking I was just feeding her bedroom lines. She had no idea how serious I really was. "Please, I need to feel you." Her alto voice was even richer when soaked in lust.

I nuzzled the inside of her thigh, trying to discover and memorize everything about her at the same time. Baby-fine blond hair dusted her skin, more visible now that she prickled with goose bumps.

I licked the spot I had been kissing and made a wet path toward her center. Her mound was silky smooth, and I wondered if she did her own waxing. I loved doing the personal service for all my subs, and I would delight in taking care of Hannah in the same way.

Maybe I could talk her into growing the hair longer and leaving it that way. It had been a long time since I'd fucked a woman with a bush, and the thought of it made my dick jump. But just fantasizing about her grocery shopping would get me hard. I was completely and utterly consumed with Hannah Rochelle Farsey.

Instinct, Mother Nature, or some other unseen force worked overtime. My decisions were being driven by pure biology, and I was no more in control of my actions than a spawning salmon swimming upstream.

Yep. That's my story, and I'm sticking to it.

The chemistry between this woman's body and mine was driving every involuntary decision. Without thinking twice, I bit her inner thigh hard enough to make her whimper.

"Good?"

"Oh my God, yes. Yes! Feels so good, Elijah. Ah!"

I smiled around the fleshy paradise between my teeth when she called out and sounded like she was choking on my name. And...the images flashing across my brain's movie screen after that thought. Her choking on my cock. My hands around her delicate throat. My monogrammed Valentino belt in the same place. Fastening her collar a few holes too tight. Using my favorite tie...

Holy. Shit. This woman was crawling into my psyche, and it was going to take a lobotomy and a crowbar to get her out.

The gathered fervor from my last mental slide show was my fuel and fire to dive into her cunt like I hadn't eaten in days. Her taste was tart and sweet at the same time—and the smell. Oh my God, the smell was scrambling the circuitry in my mind. The velvety feel of her labia and the firm but soft button at the center all combined to make the most delicious pussy I'd ever feasted on.

I licked Hannah's slit from bottom to top with my entire tongue. Then repeated the action again and again until her folds were slick and plump with her arousal. I used her own lubrication to slide one finger inside. My girl moaned so loudly from the move, I did a quick check in to make sure that was a pleasure sound and not one of pain.

"Beauty? Still good?"

"God, yes. So good. Can we ... are we ..." Hannah tried to complete her thought several times and with several different combinations of words. Finally, she got so frustrated she flopped back into the pillow pile and said nothing.

I really wanted to experience this woman's climax. Because she was so inexperienced, it would be messy, honest, and pure. The absolute best kind of orgasm to wring from a person.

Time to turn up the heat.

"Fuck, girl. This pussy is so sweet. I could eat you for every meal and die a satisfied man." I gripped into the fleshiest part of her inner thighs and wrenched her legs farther apart, purposefully emitting a very loud, greedy groan when they reached their limit. Adding a second finger inside her body, I held my breath while she adjusted and waited to see if she could handle the intrusion.

"Ooooh, Elijah. Why does that feel so good?"

"Because you're so damn tight, baby, and it feels good to be stuffed. Your body knows what it wants."

"I feel like I'm going to come."

"That's what I want to hear. Tell me what you need so I can take you there."

"I don't know. I don't know. I never did it like this. That feels really good, though, what you're doing. Oh God, yes, like that. Oh my God. I don't think I should ..."

"Oh no, you definitely should. I'm going to finger your

tight cunt until you explode on my hand. What do you think?"

"Oh— Okay."

"Say it, beautiful."

"Huh?"

"Tell me what you just agreed to," I demanded, pumping my fingers in and out of her the whole time. "I want to hear the filthy words from your pretty mouth."

Hannah thrashed her head from left to right on the pillow. "I don't remember what you said. Ooooohh, shit. Oooh my God, Elijah, please."

"I said I'm going to finger your tight cunt until you explode on my hand. You're so close, I can feel you fluttering around me. I can't wait until that's my cock."

She whimpered.

I growled.

Goddammit, I needed some relief too. Even if I came in my pants, I didn't care. The skin on my shaft was stretched so tight it felt like it would split open.

"Feel me while I finger fuck you. Squeeze, rub, whatever, I don't care. I just need to feel you. You can stop when you tell me what I'm waiting to hear, beautiful."

"Wha-What if I can't remember?" she panted.

"Then we can come together," I teased with a mischievous wink.

Seconds flew by. After Hannah felt the erection tucked away in my pants, it only took a few more deep pumps of my hand, and she came wildly. I wanted to catalog every twitch and moan, but she was so expressive, as I suspected she would be, I couldn't possibly witness every nuance.

Clearly, we'd just have to do it again and again until I was sure I'd seen everything I'd missed the times before.

As I pulled the beautiful woman close to me, and she didn't protest with a single word. She was exhausted, and in a few minutes, quiet, even breathing came from where she'd fallen asleep on my chest.

Yeah... I could get used to this.

CHAPTER TWELVE

HANNAH

"You're not my mother!" I struggled against the hands holding me and shouted again, "This is not my mother! This is not my mother!" I shouted the words they taught us in school, but no one so much as blinked an eye.

Couldn't they hear me? I was yelling as loud as my little voice could yell.

Along one wall inside the public women's bathroom, a long row of white porcelain sinks sat low in mauve Formica counters. Two basins on the end were much closer to the ground so little ones could exercise some independence and wash their own hands.

Everything was so clean.

Overhead fluorescent lights bounced off shiny chrome fixtures, porcelain toilet bowls, and sinks. Brushed stainless-steel stalls provided privacy around each toilet and a moment of peace for its user.

Through my panicked tears, I made eye contact with a woman washing her hands at one of the sinks. She didn't turn back to look at me, but I knew she saw me in the mirror right in front of her.

I made my body limp and heavy the way I did when Mommy or Daddy tried to make me walk and I was tired. I still wanted to be carried sometimes, but they were always too weighed down with my sisters.

But the woman—or was it a man? I wasn't sure because her hands felt like a daddy's hands—got really, really mad, and then my head hurt and I cried.

"Hannah. Hannah, baby, wake up."

"No, stop touching me. You are not my mother!"

"Hannah, wake up. You're having a nightmare, beautiful."

I shoved at the hands on my shoulders and swung my arms and balled fists wildly until finally connecting with something solid.

"Uugghh. Well, shit, girl."

A man. I was in bed with a man. I cracked one eye open, then the other.

Elijah.

A deep breath escaped as my brain came online, and I realized I'd just landed a solid fist to his body somewhere. I stared at the stunning man, with what I assumed were saucer-wide eyes. I'd been having various versions of the same nightmare for almost twenty years. Not an anniversary I was eager to celebrate. Or an experience I typically talked about, if I could get away with it. Now that this happened, though, I was sure I'd have to come clean with my sexy landlord.

"Are you okay?" The light on my side of the bed was already on, so he hit the switch for his side too. I took a quick peek at my watch and groaned at the time. It was already too late to hope for more sleep before having to get up for work but too early to get up and get the day started.

"I'm so sorry I ruined your sleep. I hope your day isn't too busy with meetings or whatever."

"Listen to me, girl, because this is the only time I'm going to say this. You don't owe anyone an apology for having a nightmare. Especially me." In case I wasn't sure how he truly felt from his lecture, he added a disapproving scowl. "That's ridiculous. Also, it's Sunday, so there isn't an issue. We can sleep out by the pool later if we're tired."

If only it were as simple as making time for a catnap later in the day. Something about the look on his handsome face gave me the impression he also knew that wasn't the case, but until I gifted him with my truth, he would leave well enough alone.

"If it's all the same, I'm going to go back to my room. I had an amazing time with you last night, Elijah. Thank you for everything you did for me." I shifted my eyes from left to right, embarrassed to settle on any one thing too long, and gave him a shy smile.

"Don't get bashful on me now, beautiful. I'm pretty sure my face still smells like your cunt." He held his hand up between us. "My fingers definitely do."

"Oh my God," I commented from the cradle of my palms. "Why would you say something like that?" I picked my head up and glared at him. At least we weren't dwelling on the nightmare.

"There's nothing to be embarrassed about, Hannah. What we did last night was pretty tame in the realm of sexual escapades. Plus, it all felt really great, right?"

"Yes, it did. Again, thank you."

"I didn't bring it up to coax gratitude from you, Hannah."

"Then why did you?" I began to suspect he enjoyed making me uncomfortable.

"The best way for us to learn about each other is honest conversation." He gave an easy shrug. "It's that simple. If I have to guess what you like and what you don't, I'm going to get a lot wrong. And I can say, when it comes to you, I don't want to get it wrong."

For a moment, I was speechless. "Oh. All right, then" was the best I could come up with, and when I heard myself say it, I winced. I sounded like an inexperienced teen.

"Will you answer a few questions about last night so I can make your experience even better next time?"

"What makes you think there will be a next time?"

He treated me to the puppy dog head tilt, ensuring my mouth went dry and the space between my legs was wet. After finger-combing his hair back into place, he reached for me with outstretched arms.

"What?" I asked as if I didn't understand what he wanted or needed from me.

"I would like to hold you while we talk. Is that possible? Why are you acting so cagey? The nightmare?"

"I thought you just said you weren't pissed," I said sharply.

"I'm not."

"Well, it seems like the moment I don't give in to what you want, you give me attitude."

"Nope. Definitely not."

"Hmmm."

"What's really going on here? And don't say nothing or that it's my imagination."

"I'm not really in the mood to talk about sex right now, Elijah. I think I want to go back to my room and go back to sleep after all."

He narrowed his eyes when he studied me. "What are the nightmares about? Do you want to talk about that? Is it always the same dream? You weren't too rattled when you first woke up from it, so I'm guessing you've had that dream before."

God, he wasn't going to let this go, and I should've expected this from him in the first place.

"That's very presumptuous," I bit.

"I don't know." He shrugged. "I mean, yes, it's a guess. But I think it's an educated one and a correct one."

I couldn't help but laugh. Then I laughed harder, realizing I sounded a little deranged, and it reminded me of my kind, generous friend Rio. Shit. Was this what happened in this circle of people? These men were so wrapped up in questionable activities that it drove their women batty?

You're not his woman, Hannah Rochelle.

My thoughts must have been written across my face, or maybe I was talking to myself again, because Mr. Psych 101 commented, "No, beautiful, she was nuts when she met Grant. He had nothing to do with it. If anything, he saved her from tipping the scale any further."

"How can you be so cruel? You know she's my friend, and still, you say something like that. I don't think I like you very much right now. I'm going to go to my room"—I made an up-and-over gesture—"on the other side of this ridiculously large house of yours. I'll see you later. Or not."

"Hannah, wait," he called as I walked purposefully out of the master suite.

"Do not follow me right now," I called over my shoulder with my hand up as a stop signal. And I really hoped he listened, or we were going to have a big, ugly argument.

I knew Elijah cared about my well-being, but I also knew he thought he had charm an inexperienced girl like me couldn't refuse. Where did the playboy stop and the real man begin? Was there even a difference at this point?

Routing through the kitchen, I decided to make myself a cup of tea. I grabbed some loose tea leaves from a canister I spotted in the pantry a few days ago and filled the metal ball Elijah had nearby on the same shelf. Not the organizational system I would've used, but he was a man, so I had to kick dirt over that mess and move on. With a full kettle of water on the stovetop, I had a few minutes to wait.

When I felt around in my back pocket, I realized I didn't have my phone. It had been since I napped last night, before we were to go to dinner, that I could remember having it. If anyone from my family had been trying to get a hold of me, they'd be hysterical by now. At least they had Rio's and Abbi's names and phone numbers. In a true emergency, someone would think to find me through one of them.

I hustled to my room to grab the device, and it lay on the table beside the bed. Elijah's housekeeper came through every morning and made the bed if I hadn't done so myself, so she must have set it there. Quickly, I pulled the charging cord from the wall and jogged back to the kitchen just in time to find Elijah pouring hot water into two cups. The metal chain to the loose-leaf ball I had filled dangled over the rim of one of them.

"I'm so sorry. Was it whistling? I hurried..." I thumbed over my shoulder toward my room. "It couldn't have been two minutes."

"Stop freaking out about it. It was just coming up when I walked into the room. I thought a cup of tea sounded nice. Do you mind if I join you?" He seemed a bit sheepish, and it was such a departure from his usual behavior, I had to chuckle.

"Of course not. This is your house, Elijah."

"Hannah—"

"No. Don't." I didn't want to hear about how last night was a mistake and I was supposed to just be there so he could protect me until we figured out who was in the kitchen at Abstract that day.

"You don't even know what I was going to say."

"There's nothing to say." I thought for a second or two and then changed my mind. Maybe a little contrition would go a long way with this guy.

"I'm sorry I allowed myself to become so vulnerable last night. That wasn't fair to you. You already have enough going on, and you don't need to be babysitting me, too. I mean, obviously, that's what you are doing. Babysitting me, right? I don't want to be your burden, Elijah. It's not a good feeling for me. I'm going to talk to Rio this afternoon and see if her future husband thinks it's safe for me to go home."

I could hear the way I was rambling, and based on the grin he was trying—and failing, I might add—to hide, I was pretty sure he could too.

"First of all," Elijah said, stepping around the island so we both were on the same side of the slab of stone. His voice was so dark and seductive, I thought of a predator, luring its prey into a clever trap.

Don't do the head tilt. Don't do the head tilt. Don't do the head tilt.

"Do you really not understand?" he asked calmly.

"Understand what?" My reply was burdened with impatience.

"I want you here. I want *you*." He took a step toward me, and the intense look he leveled me with was more potent than anything I'd seen from him before. "Do you understand me now, beautiful? Is that clear enough?"

"You don't have to talk to me like—"

"Do you understand me?" he growled again.

Like an insolent brat, I rolled my eyes and said, "Oh, here we go with this again."

And apparently I'd taken it a step too far with my childish response, because he was on me like the clap of thunder that follows lightning. Except I didn't even get those five seconds before he was leaning over me with his whole body, pressing my back down to the island.

"Do you understand?" he asked with his nose pressed to mine.

I pushed as hard as I could on the twin muscle stacks of his chest. "Yes! For fuck's sake, Elijah, I understand you!"

We both stood up, and I glared at him sideways as I put some distance between us.

"Are you happy? I understand every word that comes out of that sinful mouth." Tears were welling up, and I closed my eyes. I didn't want to pull an Abbi here. God, it was the last thing I wanted to do. "But what do you want from me? I'm trying to be the spineless, pliant houseguest here. I really am. You're not making it easy. If you're ever honest with yourself, you have to see that." I sagged onto one of the counter stools and put my folded hands between my thighs.

I finally looked up and found his eyes fixed on me. One fat tear rolled down my cheek.

"How do you not see I'm trying?"

"Is that really what you think I want you to be? Or do?"

"Isn't that what the other women who come through your door do? Or act like?" I shrugged. "I thought I was just the next in line."

"Beautiful girl, you are nothing—and let me say that

again—*nothing* like the women I bring here to fuck."

I winced at the crass description of his relationships. If that was what they could be called.

"So what am I, then?"

"Stunning. Fascinating. Intriguing. Of course, my favorite"—and he inserted that fucking grin—"beautiful."

"We should've never fooled around last night. It just complicated everything. I know you and your friends have some troublesome things going on. And I know I somehow got dragged into it. Wrong place at the wrong time, as far as I can tell. Let's just pretend last night never happened and go back to you making sure I'm safe and us avoiding each other outside of that. I think that's probably our best plan."

"No."

"No?"

"No. I loved every second of what happened between us yesterday. From up in the clouds to between your thighs."

While he was in the middle of that embarrassing comment, his cell phone must have vibrated in his back pocket, because he fished the thing out with efficiency and put it up to his ear in one smooth motion.

"Banks. Yeah, hey, man. What do you have for me? All right, will do. Thanks, I appreciate the weekend work. Yeah, yeah." He grinned and ended the call.

Well, what do you know? He could have a normal conversation with someone.

When he ended his call, he scrolled through his phone, and his eyes darted back and forth across the small screen and then got eerily still. He looked up to find me watching him.

Trying to interpret the expression I saw staring back from those captivating features was unnerving.

"Elijah? What is it? Is everything okay?"

He took a deep breath. "Do the names Ronald and Cynthia Trask sound familiar?"

Of course they do, but why would he know that?

I nodded slowly. Like every other time over the past twenty years, hearing those names put me in a tunnel the size of a pinpoint. I had to focus and fight to get to the other side. There was no oxygen in this tunnel. Couldn't breathe. Couldn't see.

Help me. Someone help me.

This is not my mother.

"Okay, let's sit down." Elijah's voice came across the tunnel, and I felt hands grasp my shoulders.

As per my programmed response, I batted at his chest as he approached.

"Don't touch me," I said—or tried to say through the vise grip around my throat.

The confident man eased me down to the counter stool and then gave me the space I needed.

Finally, when the panic ebbed, I looked at him through clear eyes and asked, "Who told you about this?"

"Let's go sit on the sofa, where it's more comfortable and there isn't a hard floor under you. That makes me nervous."

"Say what you need to say right here."

"Okay, you stand there, then, if that's what you prefer. I'm going to sit in there." He thumbed over his shoulder toward the great room. "I'll shout if you can't hear me. Just let me know."

"Why are you such an ass?" I asked to his back. The view of his actual ass while he did so, however, was nothing if not divine.

"Elijah Banks," I muttered, "I think I hate you." I mumbled

the whole thing under my breath, but based on the cocky smirk on his face when he scooted back into the corner seat of the sectional sofa, he heard me just fine.

With a huff, I went and sat on the sofa opposite my host and propped my elbows on my knees. I really wanted to control this narrative in just one relationship in my life. I didn't think that was too much to ask for.

"Tell me what you know," I said. "Also, why do you know about this part of my life? Those records were sealed. I was a minor."

"Let me start by asking you a question. Do you know my occupation?"

"You work at Shark Enterprises," I said with confidence, but when I tried to drill it down to what he did there, I couldn't. I gave him a little shake of my head. "I'm afraid I don't know. My guess, based on you coming to Abstract with Grant that afternoon, is it must have something to do with security."

"That's a very good and educated guess. I do a lot of background checking when new people come into Sebastian's orbit, mostly corporate-level stuff. I also have a team of hackers I work very closely with when things get questionable. I make sure Bas's security systems are tight and that no one has breached them. Well, you get the picture. It's a lot of security stuff but not limited to that. Also, not always white hat, if that's what's called for. In other words, I have the resources I need to get the job done."

"Okay, that's all great. I'm sure you have a very impressive résumé. But that doesn't answer why you have very personal information about me that I did not give you permission to obtain. I'm not in Sebastian Shark's immediate circle, and neither is this…" I made a weird hand gesture in front of me to represent the matter at hand.

"There's the rub. If you read your employment contract at Abstract, you'd know that you agreed to background checks, drug screening, stuff like that, at the employer's discretion. Because my best friend is a paranoid motherfucker, when Abbigail was in Twenty-Nine Palms last summer, everyone who ever breathed near the woman was investigated or reinvestigated. I believe you were hired when she got back, right?"

"Yes, that's right. I heard about some of that, though, from her and Rio."

"Since then, all new hires are screened by my team. When you were filmed in the cooler, I had my team do the next-tier investigation to see if there were any obvious standouts that might be after you personally. Because I was thinking—at the time, of course—that that incident may have had nothing to do with Shark. This is all pretty standard information, right? I mean, it's making sense?"

"Of course. But it still doesn't explain why you have sealed court documents."

The familiar sense of unease... No, who was I kidding? This wasn't unease. The creepy-crawly feeling on my skin would manifest into full-blown tarantulas again in the next several minutes if I didn't get a grip.

I shot up from where I was perched on the edge of the sofa cushion and started the first lap around the large open room. At that moment, I was grateful to Elijah and his castle-sized home. At least I didn't feel like an animal in a display at the zoo.

But my foolish zookeeper didn't get the memo about trying to wrestle the tiger when she was looking a bit feral.

Elijah stepped in front of me on lap two and gripped my forearms.

Yanking from his grasp, I could tell I totally surprised him by the strength I truly possessed. "Not now, Banks," I growled.

Hands went up like he'd just been caught trying to hot-wire one of the fancy cars in this neighborhood. "All right. All right. Tell me how to help you. It's torture watching you like this."

"Then answer my damn question! How. Do. You. Have. That. Information?"

"I want you to tell me what those people mean to you. The whole story. That way, I will know how to handle the small bit of information I have. Because, beautiful, I think your world is about to be turned upside down, and I want to be the one there to catch you when you fall."

I sagged back down onto the sofa and cradled my face in my hands. He had no idea how wrong he was. If I told him what had happened when I was just a little girl, how it'd followed me around my whole life, rerouted every decision my entire family ever made, he wouldn't want me around. I was the world's biggest burden. He just didn't know it yet.

I looked up to see him studying me closely, looking like he was cataloging every breath I took, every molecule of mine that shifted in space.

Tears ran hot and furious down my cheeks.

Hey, check it out! I was an animal on display after all.

And I was about to lose the best thing I ever had. And why did it hurt like he was mine to lose?

Elijah came to me and sank to his knees on the floor in front of me. Like the bossy ass he was, he growled—no shit, *growled*—and pushed at my knees until I spread my legs and made room for him to get closer. When he wrapped his capable and comforting arms low around my hips, I let him. I just let him. Because it would likely be the last time he showed me any sort of kindness or affection like this, and I just wanted to savor the gentle safety of this overbearing, sexy bastard for a little longer.

I ran my fingers through his tousled sandy-brown hair over and over, letting the motion calm me.

When my heart wasn't beating in my throat and my breathing settled back to something resembling a normal rhythm, I put on the bravest voice I could. A whisper seemed all I was capable of at the moment, and I could acknowledge nothing really sounded brave while spoken at that volume. But it was all I had left.

These people stole my life. Even though they were never successful with their intention, they stole it all.

Intention.

I loathed that word in this scenario.

Deep breath in, and on the exhale, I trusted him with my biggest vulnerability. What he did with it after, well … time would tell.

"I was five years old, almost six." I smiled, remembering how excited I had been.

Elijah studied me closely while I told my story, taking in every facial expression and cataloging every shift in weight.

"My mom always made such a big deal about our birthdays. It was the one day we had all to ourselves. With so many sisters, it was easy to get lost in the shuffle, especially since I was the oldest."

When I didn't say anything for a few moments, Elijah leaned back farther to directly meet my gaze.

"Do you want to get up off your knees?" I asked. "That can't be comfortable."

He leaned in, and his stubble scraped my ear when he spoke. In his seductive, painfully promising growl he said, "If we weren't in the middle of a very serious conversation, I would show you how long I can spend in this position." He leaned back again and gave me one of those naughty winks accompanied by the lazy, sultry grin.

That mischievous smile was my favorite of all the tricks he had in his lady-killer toolbox. Damn thing worked on me every time.

"I'm sorry I interrupted. But it's a little distracting being so close to your pussy."

"Sit up here, then." I patted the sofa cushion beside me while grinning. "Or go back over there where you started."

"I'll sit there if you join me," he countered.

I looked at him quizzically, so he tugged me to stand, and we crossed the seating area to his coveted corner spot in the sectional, where he arranged his body against the two sides and then held his arms open to me in invitation.

"Isn't this defeating the purpose of rearranging?"

"I'll be good. I promise. If you feel my dick poking you, though, it can't be helped. We both just have to resign ourselves to that fact."

Giving in to his idea, I crawled between his legs, thinking how much better it would be to fool around than spill my guts to him. I knew my shirt's neckline hung open enough that he should be getting a free view of my unrestrained breasts.

The masculine groan that came from him confirmed my suspicion.

"Girl, I only have so much willpower. After last night, it's down by half."

With hands planted on the outside of his hips, I leaned over him and kissed his full lips. Lightly at first to see if he would join me or reject me.

Between kisses I asked, "Half?"

"At least," Elijah answered in a voice rougher than I'd ever heard from another person. He cradled my face in his hands and kissed me soundly but pulled back way too soon. "I know if we don't stop now, I'm going to have you beneath me in my bed again, beautiful. This is too important to you, to me, and to us, to blow off in favor of sex."

I let my chin drop to my chest with a disappointed sigh and said, "I know you're right."

"Sit with me here and finish your story. We'll take it from there."

That quickly, that easily, he made me feel like he was in control of the situation. And for this quiet moment inside his house, he was.

After we got situated, Elijah urged me to continue talking. Absentmindedly, I toyed with his fingers while I spoke.

"We were living in Orange County at the time. My dad is a CPA—I don't know if I ever told you that?" I turned a little in his arms to look at him but realized how silly that was. He was a damn spy just about. He probably knew this whole story already. Why was I having to go through the pain of reliving it?

"Do you already know what happened? I mean, you have sneaky ways of finding things out, apparently. You probably know all about this nightmare." Instantly I felt like an accusatory bitch, but I couldn't help it. I hated having to relive this. It had been the single worst day of my life, and I lived with the trickle-down effects from it every day. Like drops from a mountainside spring, it eroded the rocks that formed my family, my parents' marriage, my whole fucking life that should've been.

That could've been.

"No, I don't know what happened. I saw the rap sheet for those pieces of shit and then saw your name and immediately closed the file. I don't think you are grasping how much I care about you, Hannah. I know we haven't known each other long, and I know it probably sounds like I'm feeding you bullshit to get into your pants. You know I have some painful and complicated history with a woman, and you've been very respectful and not asked about it."

"Elijah, that's not my business until you want it to be. I, of all people, understand that."

"And I, of all people, understand the same about your past. I hope you will give me this gift."

"Gift? Beautiful man, how is this dumpster fire a gift?"

"The gift is you trusting me enough to help you carry the burden. Do you understand that?"

"Oh, no. Don't do it. Don't you dare."

"What?"

"Don't do the"—I dropped my voice as low as it could possibly go to try to imitate his, furrowed my brow, and attempted a menacing, dominant glare—"*do you understand me* bit. Yes. I understand you. Sometimes you have to give me longer than one inhalation to answer."

My God. I thought I'd seen this man at his most compelling before, but none of his alluring facets had compared to watching or simply hearing Elijah Banks laugh. Authentically laugh.

When he recovered from that much-needed break, I slung my arms around his neck and looked into his mesmerizing hazel eyes. They were less icy today. Studying this man's face could be a fine-arts class at the college up the street.

"How is this happening?" I asked him suspiciously. I was trying to guard my heart, but with every day I spent near him, the more flank I exposed.

"When you come up with an answer, will you let me know?" He then melted me to my needy, aching core with a kiss so passionate, I whimpered when he pulled away.

"Do we have to stop? I could spend hours kissing you."

"Hmmm, I like the sound of that, beauty. How about this, though? Because I think it's vital you finish telling me this information. Something is making the hair on the back of my neck stand up about that report my men put together, and I haven't even read the whole thing yet. That can't be good. But once we get all this shitty stuff out of the way, we have the whole day to do whatever we feel like doing."

"All right. I like the sound of that. Incentive, or reward, maybe?"

"Exactly."

CHAPTER THIRTEEN

ELIJAH

I was going to kill someone. Or a pair of someones. I had to keep my features on par with the story as she recounted it, or it would be obvious I was letting my carefully controlled temper get the better of me. I spent hours each day—well, before she moved in—practicing techniques of mindfulness, calmness, and qi alignment so I didn't end up in prison beside people like these two.

Only two people on the planet knew I should've been there on my own merit. If I were lucky, one was dead by now, but I had no way of knowing without investigating, and I'd be damned if I'd even give him that satisfaction. The other was a woman I was quickly and finally putting in my rearview mirror.

Hannah lay in my arms, absentmindedly toying with my fingers while I buried my face in her soft hair. I imagined what it would be like to spend an evening this way after a long day at the office. We could take turns making dinner or spend time in the kitchen doing it together. Then after, curl up like this and watch a movie or read . . .

Hannah's alto voice cut into my daydream. It was better anyway. I needed to be present for her, especially right now.

"I don't think he'd made partner yet, so we hadn't moved to Los Angeles. My mom didn't have a nanny or any help from family, so if she needed to do errands, we all went along. We went to Target to get stuff for my birthday party, and my mom had her hands full with the twins." She laughed. "Who am I kidding? She always did. We should've known then already that Sheppard was going to be a pain in the ass. God, Elijah, that girl cried so much when she was little. Everything, seriously, everything . . . made her cry."

She stopped talking for a minute, and I wondered what she was thinking about.

"What is it?" I asked.

"I was just thinking of the other night again. When I went over to the house after work. She was so ugly to me. If she's in a lousy mood and I'm around, I'm the one in her crosshairs. But, anyway, back to the story at hand. We were in the store— me, Agatha, and the twins, Sheppard and Maye. I wandered off down the next aisle, and my mom didn't even notice because, like I said, the babies were crying.

"It all happened so quickly. Someone grabbed me from behind, and it wasn't until we were in the restroom that I saw their faces. There was someone waiting for us in the bathroom, and the person who took me from the aisle stripped my clothes off. I remember I had a pink dress on that day and these sandals I loved. My mom hated them because the one always fell off my foot at the worst times, you know? In the middle of a parking lot, or in a restaurant, and we'd have to go back to see if anyone found it and turned it in."

"It sounds like you have a really good mom," I said wistfully, wondering what my own mother would've done. Sent one of the staff to find the sandal, I was sure.

"I really do. But she's beat herself up mercilessly every day since this happened."

"So, I'm guessing they changed your clothes in the restroom? You must have been terrified."

"Yes and no. I don't remember a lot of it, and I have refused to watch the security footage. I think since I don't have the memory myself, why would I want to inject that into my brain? I don't know if that makes sense. To some people it does, and to others it doesn't. My therapist says if that's how I want it to be, that's all that matters."

"It sounds like you have a really good therapist. And I'm already breathing easier knowing you've gotten therapy after something like this." I only imagined how much worse this story was about to get.

"I do. Her name is Ellen. I don't see her routinely anymore unless I'm having problems with something, and then I get back on a schedule immediately. I've tried doing things on my own before, and it didn't go so well."

"There's nothing wrong with having a support team."

"Agreed. So the one gave me an injection of something while the other one cut my hair off so I wouldn't be immediately identified as a little girl in a pink dress with long blond hair. Now I looked like a little boy with short hair in shorts and a T-shirt."

I was tamping down outrage. As calmly as possible, I asked, "And no one saw any of this going on? There was no one else in that bathroom?"

Hannah started nodding, already sensing my agitation and wanting to calm it. I'd noticed it was her immediate response when she knew someone else was upset. Unruffle them first. Always the other person first.

"There was one woman. I remember seeing her, and I kept yelling that this was not my mom, because they taught us that in school. The woman looked at me in the mirror, but I was later made to understand she acted like she was just minding her own business so she could safely get out of the bathroom and get help."

Hannah sucked in a deep breath through her nose and blew it out through tight lips, then admitted, "That was always very hard to understand as a child. How could a mom-looking woman just stand there and not help me? You know?" She took another deep breath. "So still, now, when I retell this messed-up story, that sticks in here." She thumped on her chest.

"Do you want some water or something? Need to take a break?" I rubbed my hands along her arms.

"No, it's fine. I'm almost done. They closed off all the exits, and when the two people, who turns out were a man and woman, not two women like my child mind perceived, tried to leave the store with me sleeping on the man's shoulder from whatever drug they injected me with, my mom saw them and knew it was me and was able to identify me."

"Oh, thank God." I spun her so fast on my lap, I nearly toppled her to the floor. I had no idea that was how this story was going to end, and I felt the relief as if she had been mine. "Oh, Hannah, thank fucking God."

"Hey. Hey," she said, hugging me and rubbing my back. "It's okay, Elijah . . ."

I couldn't loosen my hold on her. Not yet. So, instead, I just kept murmuring into her neck, "Thank God, beautiful. Thank God."

Finally, I pulled back to look at her beautiful, all-natural face. I knew what she saw when she looked at me. I could feel the moisture on my cheeks, and I didn't care if she saw that I cried for her. I had no problem crying when the occasion called for it, and I was so thankful she hadn't endured days—or longer—of torture, molestation, or other kinds of sick, fucked-up abuse.

"Look at you," I said. "Comforting me. This is so ass-backwards." I shook my head in disbelief. How had this woman stumbled into my life?

Please, I am begging you, God, whoever . . . don't let me fuck this one up.

"Do you know what caught my mom's attention when they were walking past her with their supposed child sleeping on the man's shoulder?"

"What?" I asked, my voice still thick with emotion.

"It was that damn sandal. The one had fallen off, and the other was still securely on my foot. The Trasks weren't parents and hadn't even noticed. But my mom saw it immediately and knew, regardless of the clothes and hair, that it was me. She knew."

"That's incredible," I said in awe. "See? I knew you had a really great mom." I didn't know what more I could add.

"My mom still has that shoe to this day," Hannah said with so much pride. And for the first time since recounting the horrid tale, tears welled in her eyes. "Damn, almost made it without crying."

I pulled her close again, and she climbed back into my lap with her entire body. With my face buried in her hair, I gently rocked her. Now I needed to figure out what to do with the information in the report sitting in my email inbox. While what I'd told Hannah was true, I'd seen enough of it when put together with everything she just shared with me to know a shitstorm was about to rain down on her life.

First order of business should probably be talking to my

best friends and getting their take on the situation. I didn't think this would circle back to the bullshit with the pirates, but stranger things had happened where Sebastian was involved. There was a large part of me that was shocked Hannah hadn't insisted I tell her what was in that file the moment she shared her history. Another thought popped into mind, and how I hadn't thought of it before, I hadn't a clue.

Why had her parents kept this information from her? As much as it sucked, I wouldn't do the same thing. She had a right to know.

"Beautiful, sit up for a second. I want to look at that email about the Trasks. My mind has latched on to something I saw that's not making sense. I need to connect the dots."

"Are you hungry?" she asked. "I don't know about you, but that tea only went so far, and now I'm starving. Why don't I go make us something to eat while you do what you need to do? How does an omelet sound?"

"That sounds perfect. I can't skip a workout again today. I gotta keep in shape for my lady."

"Your lady?" she teased from a few feet away. At least, I thought she was teasing. "Is that right?" she pressed me for more as she came within reaching distance.

"Yes, that's damn right." I snaked my arm out from where I sat on the sofa and grabbed her around the backs of the thighs and pulled her to stand between my knees. I pulled up her T-shirt enough to expose a strip of bare skin that I could press my lips to.

"I told you before, once I'm with a woman, I'm only with that woman." Then it dawned on me. What if she didn't want a relationship? "I just assumed you wanted the same thing I did, but now I'm wondering if I'm making a jackass out of myself."

"Elijah Banks. I have to say, you're pretty adorable when you're nervous."

I pinched her ass to remind her who was still in charge. "Adorable I can live with. Behind closed doors, at least. Nervous? Never."

Now that she'd planted the thought of food, I was starving. I could look at the email in a few minutes. I picked Hannah up effortlessly and carried her in a front piggyback to the kitchen and set her on the island.

"An omelet, huh? Anything sound better?"

"Hmmm . . ." She made a big show of thinking and then put her index finger straight up in the air. "You," she said, laughing with that throaty husk that had driven me insane since the first time I heard it.

Fixing my stare to hers first, I prowled back to her, leaving the refrigerator wide open. Well, she had my attention now. Quickly, I stood before my beauty and tried to push my way between her legs, but she squeezed her thighs together.

Oh, she had no idea how I loved a good struggle in the bedroom. But considering all the information shared over the past couple of hours, I knew we needed to have a careful and detailed conversation about bedroom triggers. In the meantime, I'd have to curb my urges and play on the safe side of the line.

I leaned past her so I could speak low and directly into her ear. "My house. My woman. My pussy. Mine." I bit her earlobe to punctuate my point.

Next, I moved down to the graceful slope where her neck met her shoulder and bit there too.

Her sensual moan was met with my declaration, "Mine."

Finally, I trailed wet kisses outward along her collarbone

to the ball of her shoulder. There, after sinking in for a third bite, I finished with the verbal claim, "Mine."

"Elijah..." she gasped, but when I moved directly in front of her again, she didn't finish the thought. I loved the notion that I was overwhelming her with pleasure. Just from a few nibbles and seductive promises, she couldn't string a whole sentence together, and it fed my ego in the best way.

"Yeah, baby?"

But she didn't respond. She just stared into my eyes with her glassy ones and with a beautiful flush high on her cheeks.

"Have you decided what you want to eat?" I asked. "How do you feel about quiche?"

"Can you make that? If you say yes, I think I'm going to go pack my things and leave. You can't look like this, have a body like you do, be...well...you know...like you are in the bedroom, and I'm sure you're outstanding at your job too."

I cut off her rambling by suggesting, "Why don't you help me? We can do it together."

"Oh, I like that idea. I'm not very good at being waited on. I'd much rather be useful."

"But letting people do things for you doesn't negate your usefulness."

"In my rational mind I know that, but my anxious brain doesn't always take a back seat long enough for the rational side to be in charge. I think that's why I gravitated to food prep for a career."

"Explain."

"Well, it's so fast-paced, day or night, that you don't have time to obsess over silly things. You just get in there and get it done. It's when I have too much time on my hands, too much time to think, that my mind starts messing with me."

"I think we're all like that to a certain degree, don't you?"

"I'm not really sure. I only know my own brain. Elijah, you have to understand something. I haven't been in long-term relationships with other men by design."

"I'm guessing because of what happened? What you just told me? But, Hannah, you were a child. None of what happened was your fault."

"I know that, but it's changed who I am now. Everything in my life has been rewired because of that one incident. Something that happened twenty years ago, that took less than three hours out of the whole of my life, changed everything. Changed me, my parents, my siblings, my friendships. Everything."

"Do you want to talk about it more?"

"I don't know. Do you? I don't want to bore you with it all. I know when anyone goes on and on about themselves it can be a bit much, so it's as much up to you as it is me."

"Beautiful, I love learning all there is to know about you. How many eggs do we need?"

"Six should be good. Oh, wait, we need to make the pie crust first."

"I think I have some in the freezer. Let me check."

"Elijah Banks. My grandmother would tan my hide if she found out I used a frozen pie crust."

"Did you just say tan your hide? Girl, where are your relatives from? Isn't that a southern expression?"

She laughed, and just like every other time, it shot straight to my cock and stroked me to a quick erection. I closed my eyes for a moment and hung my head until my chin hit my chest.

Think unsexy thoughts. Don't picture her pussy. Or her perfect tits. Or your dick sliding between them.

"You okay over there?"

"Getting there," I groaned.

"What's wrong? Is it all that stuff from my past? See, this is what I'm talking about. It gets overwhelming before you even realize what's happening."

"No, that's not it. Not even close."

"What's wrong, then?"

I went to stand in front of her and took her hands in mine. Keeping direct eye contact, I put her hands over my swollen crotch.

"Oh, Jesus," Hannah muttered, eyes gone cartoonishly wide.

"See the problem now? Or feel it, more accurately? Your laugh has this husky, throaty quality, and this is the direct result on my body."

Shocking me completely, she squeezed a bit and ran her hand along the length, exploring my cock with much more bravery than I expected.

"Elijah. That's never going to...I mean...how...I don't..."

I knew what she was getting worked up about, and I had to set her fears to rest. Things would work. I'd been down the exact road she was worried about many times before.

"It will work just fine. We have to work into it. You just have to trust me, okay?"

The whole time I was talking, she was jacking my dick, and I couldn't bear asking her to stop. It felt so fucking good, I wanted to yank my pants down and have her do it in truth.

"Can I feel your skin?" she asked, tentatively running one hand along my waistband while the other still rubbed the front of my joggers.

"I don't know if that's such a good idea, beautiful. Plus, weren't we going to make breakfast? Oh, shit, that feels good. I'm going to need a couple of minutes to handle this, though. There's no way it's going to go away on its own now."

"I want to watch you."

"You're full of surprises this morning, Ms. Farsey." I thought for a moment or two and decided on a plan.

"Get a pillow off the sofa in the other room and come back." While she scurried off like her heels were on fire, I got the olive oil out of the pantry. We would need it for the breakfast anyway. Hannah was back in a flash, gripping the pillow like a life preserver.

"Are you sure?" I asked her. I didn't want to push her too far, too fast, but the minute she planted the idea, it grew into a full, living, throbbing fantasy.

"Yes, I want this," she answered with quiet confidence.

I held out my hand, she offered the cushion she'd just retrieved, and I dropped it in the middle of the kitchen floor.

"Kneel…" I pointed and then gave her my hand for balance while she got into position.

"Hannah, look at me." I waited for her to meet my stare because it was important that she understood her well-being would always be my number-one concern.

Through the curtain of light-brown lashes, her blue eyes found mine.

I stepped closer to put my hand beneath her chin. My God, she couldn't possibly know how natural she looked in this pose. My dick swelled impossibly harder for her. I crouched down in front of her, still holding her chin in the cup of my palm.

"At any time, no matter when we're together or what we're

doing—whether we're talking or fucking or playing Go Fish—at any time, if you need a break or to stop completely, all you have to do is say slow or stop, and we will. I'm not into doing things against your will"—I ticktocked my head and grinned—"unless that's the kind of game we're playing. Then we will renegotiate beforehand. But these are the general rules, okay?"

"Okay. Thank you for telling me that."

"You're welcome, beauty." I stood to my full height and took one step back so I could drink in all her perfection. "Take off your shirt."

Her head jerked up, proud chin leading the charge of defiance.

Maybe I misread her desire for submission, but I wasn't usually wrong about recognizing the trait in a woman.

A sound of warning came from low in my throat. We could push and pull a bit and see where it took us. Sometimes the woman craved that bit of icing on the cake as much as I did. In fact, most of my early experiences were what led me to my current preferences.

"I don't ask twice, beautiful," I warned. "Are you so eager for punishment already?"

"I just thought—"

"Did I say you could speak?"

"Did you say I couldn't?" she shot back.

Well, shit. She had a point there, and I couldn't help but chuckle. We were going to have a lot of fun. I could tell that much. Hannah was not only beautiful—my dream girl—but she was smart and quick-witted.

Yeah, my dream girl.

I thought I'd let my dream girl slip through my grasp years ago. But the more time I spent around Hannah Farsey, the more I was starting to think Hensley Pritchett wouldn't hold a candle to this woman in any category. Time would tell if I was right or not, but years of maturity and learning about myself and the world around me had all signs pointing in that direction. I had to figure out a way to keep my wits about me, though, so I didn't go overboard and scare her away.

"Are you going to do it, or do you want me to do it for you?" I asked.

"You" was all she said in way of reply.

All right. Hopefully she didn't mind my methods. I closed the distance between us faster than she could track and put my large hands in the neckline of her shirt. After one forceful motion, the fabric hung in two pieces off her arms and her beautiful tits were fully exposed. I already had my back to her, making my way back to my starting point as if the whole encounter was inconsequential. Truth be told, I could not wait to pivot and get an eyeful of my handiwork.

I honestly didn't know what was more priceless. The look on her face or her bare breasts.

Fine, it was her tits, but just barely.

"Don't push me, beauty. It usually ends better for me than you."

"Do you have any idea how shitty my salary is? You're such an asshole for doing that."

"Careful now, unless you like soap in your mouth."

"What?"

"Don't call me names, or you will have a mouthful of come or soap, and I'm guessing a good girl like you is going to pick soap."

"You don't know jack about me being a good girl or not."

"Are you saying you've been lying to me about your

history? Because we may not have covered a lot of rules yet, but I know we've covered that one."

"You're infuriating. Just get your dick out. Isn't that what this was supposed to be about in the first place?"

I was back in her face in a flash. So quick, in fact, she toppled backward and broke her pretty kneeling pose, landing on her backside with a thump.

Crouching down in front of her again, I tilted my head to the side, and my hair fell carelessly in front of one eye.

A little growl came from my beautiful girl, and I grinned, remembering that she liked when my hair did that.

"What's wrong, baby?" I taunted her and stood.

"Nothing. Nothing at all," she said defiantly.

"Back up on your knees."

Only, this time when I offered her assistance, she huffed and got into position on her own.

"I can tell this stubbornness is going to get you in trouble time and time again. Spread a bit, baby." I tapped the outside of one knee with my foot, and she did not like that one bit. I wasn't sure what had her so pissed, but we would talk about everything afterward.

I stroked along the outside of one pretty breast, and she inhaled greedily through her nose as I did the same to the other breast. With my whole palm, I swept underneath her full cup, testing the weight and then scraping my nails into her flesh when I released her.

"You know, I was never that much of a tits guy, but I think you might be converting me. These are amazing."

She narrowed a glare at me, so I pinched a rose-colored nipple between a thumb and index finger with both hands and glared back. I applied more and more pressure and waited for her to tap out. It was a good way to see if she absorbed what I told her about ending an activity she wasn't comfortable with or wasn't enjoying.

I had to give her credit. She took much more than I expected her to before she said very calmly, "Elijah, Sir, whatever... Slow. You're hurting me."

I was so fucking proud of her, I mauled her with my mouth. One quick kiss on the lips, and then I quickly switched to her nipple to lavish the bud with my tongue before swapping sides. While I worked one side with my mouth, I massaged the saliva into the other with my fingertips and a combination of varied pressure.

Hannah moaned and writhed beneath my ministrations until I asked her, "Are you close, beauty? Can you come like this?"

"It feels like I'm going to. It feels so good. Oh my God."

"Can I put my fingers in your cunt again? Are you sore?"

"God, yes! Please." She moaned so loudly, her answer took a few laps around the kitchen on an echo before settling in my ears.

I slid my hand into her panties and was shocked by how wet she was. Shocked and boorishly proud.

"Pull these down to your knees and leave them there. I want to see how wet you made your panties while I finger fuck you."

Feverishly, she yanked at her little bikini underwear and left them as instructed.

"Fuck yes, look at you. My God, you're so fucking hot, Hannah. Look down at what's going on here."

My gorgeous blond bombshell angled her torso the way I told her and moaned.

With all four fingertips coated in her cream, I began rubbing her clit without mercy. I knew she was right on the edge of climax—and I wasn't far off myself, just from bringing her pleasure. I sucked a nipple before giving in and biting down, figuring out she liked a little pain as long as it was quickly soothed away by pleasure. My brain was so fogged over with lust, though, it was hard to keep the lines from blurring.

"Elijah, oh God, oh shit, I'm going to come." She looked up at me with an expression of almost panic, and even that was a turn-on.

"Go, girl. Do it. Come for me, beautiful."

"God, shit, feels so good," she whispered and sagged into my embrace. I was happy to hold her and lazily swirl my fingers around her pussy until she squeaked in protest from being too sensitive.

"What about you?" Hannah asked in that husky voice that strangled my cock like a tight fist.

"It's okay," I said roughly.

"I want to see you come too," she tried to convince me.

"Oh, give it time, beauty. You'll see it plenty." I chuckled.

But Hannah reached between our bodies to find my stiff cock. "Please, let me?"

"I'll make you a deal. You can watch. How's that? After watching you just now, I think I'll take about thirty seconds." I rubbed myself through my pants and hissed. I'd had an erection for so long it actually ached.

I reached behind my head, hooked my thumb into the neckline of my T-shirt, and whipped it over my head. Straightening it out, I laid the shirt down and had my beautiful girl lie on her back on the floor before me, repurposing the pillow she'd been kneeling on to cushion her head.

"How's that? Comfortable?" I winked as I looked down at her, and she gave me an eager nod and licked her lips, pulling a groan all the way from down in my balls.

I pulled my joggers down around my thighs, and my dick sprang free from the confinement of the fabric as though giving a sigh of relief, knowing it was finally going to get a release from all the built-up tension.

Hannah propped herself on the triangle of her bent arm to have a better view, and I decided I'd allow her repositioning for now.

"You're going to want to lie down when I come, because I'm marking you, sweetheart, and unless you want a facial, you'll go back the way I arranged you."

"Fair enough," she said with a grin. "I appreciate the heads-up."

"Bend your knee, baby. Let me see . . . Fuck yes, like that." I squeezed a little tighter, pulled a little harder. The head of my cock was so dark and sensitive, and each time I thrust my hips a little rougher to push through my fist, I got closer. Closer. Closer. As predicted, I felt my stomach coiling and had zero interest in pulling back to make the shit last. I needed to come so badly, it broke free with a bite.

"Fuck yes," I hissed.

Ribbons of white, thick, milky semen shot onto Hannah's tits and belly and across the smooth mound of her pubic bone. One last thrust, and the spurt hit the top of one thigh, and I shuddered and exhaled fully for the first time in two weeks. I dropped to my hands and knees over her perfect body and tried to wrestle my heart back into the confines of my rib cage.

But it wasn't physical fitness causing the challenge in that moment. I was as fit as I'd ever been.

No, my heart knew it had found a new home, and it was no longer listening to any manner of reason from me.

CHAPTER FOURTEEN

HANNAH

The next few days went by relatively quietly. Elijah had to go out of town to do the bidding of his boss, Sebastian Shark, and no matter what question I asked regarding the trip, I netted a similar result: "It's better if we don't talk about this stuff here at the house." Or my absolute favorite, as well as insulting answer: "Contractually, I'm really not at liberty to discuss the nature of the business I do for Bas."

Well, okay, then.

I wasn't really sure what that meant, but when I brought it up to Rio, she made a very unladylike sound that could only be described as a snort and said something along the lines of, "Get used to it, sister."

I wasn't sure what to make of that comment, but I knew I didn't care for it.

While he was gone, he called or texted when he could, and each night, he would video chat with me, either on my laptop or on my cell phone. It always got me spun up sexually, no matter how we spoke.

This man was quickly digging a tunnel straight through to that place in my chest I'd protected from every other suitor my entire life. I wasn't sure how he'd managed to find a direct route there in such a short time, but I felt like a mooning teenager.

I still hadn't told him about the phone calls I'd been getting or how they were now coming daily. The person on the other end of the line was getting more brazen and starting to speak—although trying to disguise their voice. I considered bringing that up to Rio, too, but figured she had enough to juggle in her own life. Between running Abstract Catering and dealing with her own family drama with the Sharks, it was best to just handle my own dirty laundry. I was missing my family something fierce, though.

After work on Thursday, I considered a visit to my parents' house. Seeing my sisters would've been perfect to pick up my mood, but after the nonsense I endured with Shep last time I was there, I thought I'd ask Elijah if I could have Agatha come over to his place instead.

As if he could hear me thinking about him, my cell phone rang with my favorite landlord's number on the display. I picked up the call over my car's Bluetooth while I made my way toward Malibu.

"I was just thinking about you," I said, smiling. Thankfully, I'd opted to keep the convertible top up today so I could hear him without pulling over first.

"Were you thinking how happy you were going to be to see me when you got home?" he asked, and I swore I could hear the smile in his voice. Fine, maybe I imagined that part, but it was my phone call, and I'd fantasize how I'd like.

Bouncing in the bucket seat while I drove, I squealed, "Are you back? Really and truly?"

"Really and truly."

"Oh, that's awesome news. God, I can't wait to see you ... and smell you. I love the way you smell. Have I told you that?"

"No, I don't think you have, but you can say it again

when you get here. But Christ, Han, slow the fuck down. You're not at Pomona, girl."

"What? What are you talking about?"

Elijah had taken to calling me Han when he wasn't calling me some iteration of beautiful, and it made my grin get impossibly wider.

"You forget you have one of my guys on your tail in a giant SUV, and they can't whip through traffic the way you do in that little car of yours. You give Lorenzo a heart attack every time you get on the freeway."

"I'll try to be more mindful. Please tell Lorenzo I'm sorry," I offered with sincerity.

"Well, I think he thinks you're pretty, so he'll probably forgive you in short order."

"I'll flash him a little boob next time I have something low-cut on. How's that?"

"Don't you dare, or your ass will be so red you wouldn't be able to sit for a week."

Taunting him had become more fun since he'd been away. "Oh really?"

"Don't test me, beauty."

"All right, settle down, Mr. Growly Pants. Jeez. I'll see you in like ten minutes."

"Can't wait."

And then he was gone, but my stupid smile stayed in place until I pulled onto his street. Strangely, there was a car I didn't recognize blocking my way into the garage. I pulled over to the curb, and Lorenzo was out of his SUV and at my door before I could even formulate a plan as to where else to park.

"Ms. Farsey, please stay in your car. Marc is coming to accompany you to street parking until we find out what she's doing here."

"She? You know who that car belongs to?" I asked the security guard.

Before he could answer, Marc was getting in my passenger door and telling me to drive up the street and turn left at the next block.

I knew damn well that turn would take me back out onto the major road we exit the freeway onto. It was not a neighborhood street, and it wasn't the quickest way to turn around to head back toward the house in search of street parking.

"Okay, but whose car is that?" I tried the question with this guy instead.

"Please, Hannah, Ms. Farsey, pardon, if you'll just pull up to the next street and hang a left, you can turn around more easily." He pointed his meaty index finger straight out my windshield, which was unnecessary, and we both knew it.

The entire security brigade knew I was familiar with the neighborhood at this point and that I didn't need blow-by-blow instructions or a fucking personal escort in my car with me. Something was going on, and they didn't want me going inside the house.

I slammed on the brakes of my little 1 series and lit up the tires the length of half the block. The skin on Marc's face was as white as Rio's, the poor guy. But cheers to BMW and their zeal for safety equipment.

That seat belt held Marc's big body like a mother's womb. The dude looked like he had morning sickness, too.

"Stop fucking with me right now and tell me who is in that house with my man and why you all are acting like this is my first day in this neighborhood."

"Listen, I appreciate your concern for Mr. Banks. I do.

But I need this job. My wife is about to have our first child, and I can't afford to go home and tell her I got fired today. Since he's the one I work for, and he's the one who told me to get you as far away from that house until he calls and tells me to bring you back, that's what I'm going to do, even if I have to subdue you and drive this little clown car out of this neighborhood myself."

With the best glare I could muster, I narrowed my focus on Marc and seethed.

"No offense intended, ma'am," he continued.

"Cut the shit, Marc. And congratulations on the baby. What are you expecting? Where should I drive to?"

"I think anywhere that isn't that house or that street should be fine. We're having a boy. First grandson on both sides, so our parents have been relentless, you know?"

The big guy laughed and was instantly relaxed and amicable. We chatted about kids and families and just drove with no destination until his cell phone rang and we both jumped from the interruption.

"Sorry," I said and patted over my heart a few times.

The security guard whipped out his phone and spoke quickly and quietly and did a lot more listening and nodding than anything else before ending the call.

"We can head back. The problem has been secured. Mr. Banks said he will explain everything when we get back to the house."

"Well, Marc, I'm sorry, but we're at least thirty minutes away from home now, and it's also quitting time, so I think you're going to be late for dinner tonight."

"Oh, no, it's fine, Ms. Farsey. I just came on shift about an hour before all that excitement started. My workday isn't over until you and Mr. Banks are fast asleep."

As expected, it took a while to get home. Once we pulled onto Elijah's street, we passed two Malibu police cruisers heading in the opposite direction. Marc gave the officers a friendly wave, and they returned the gesture.

I didn't have time to think about it further as I pulled through the heavy gate at the end of the driveway and saw my gorgeous landlord waiting in the open garage. He stepped aside so I could pull into my usual spot, and I barely had the engine turned off before he had my door open and pulled me into his embrace.

"Are you okay?" I rushed out.

"I missed you," he said, nuzzling his face in my hair until he found the skin of my neck.

"I missed you more." I pulled back and held his handsome face between my flat palms. "But you have some explaining to do, mister."

Elijah covered my mouth with his, and I was dragged under by the magic of his lips and tongue and the sinful way he used them.

"Oh no, you don't, man. Please tell me what just happened. I want to kiss and be naked with you as soon as possible—trust me—sooner, even. But that scared me, and I don't like being kept in the dark. I'm supposed to be staying here with you so I'm safe. It doesn't feel safe to me when no one will tell me what's going on."

After I finished my little rant, he pulled me into his embrace and held me close to his hard body until we shared the same breathing pattern. The man had figured out it was an effective way of getting me to settle down when I was agitated, and I never complained because it was a win-win situation for me.

When he loosened his circle of containment, I tilted my face up to make eye contact again.

"Did you know Marc's wife is about to have their first baby? It's a boy, and you should see that big man go all squishy teddy bear when he talks about it. It's freaking adorable. I know that's random, but I ramble when I'm nervous, but you know that about me, and..."

"Hannah, stop."

So I did. Then I made the motion of locking my lips and throwing the key over my shoulder, and Elijah chuckled.

"Now, let's not get carried away. I have plans for this mouth," he said, using the pad of his thumb to drag my lower lip down as far as it would possibly go before allowing it to slip free and snap back into place. Then he gave me that sexy, smoldering *come-fuck-me* look he had perfected.

"And how can I shove my cock between these pretty lips if you lock them closed?" He tilted his head, and damn it, the hair flopped in obedience. "Although..." He made a charade of thinking. "I used to break into people's cars when I was a street urchin. I was really, reeeaally good at picking locks, as a matter of fact." He followed that comment with the panty-melting grin.

Didn't he know he didn't have to pull out the tricks with me? I would strip off my panties and throw them at him if he just suggested it.

"You're dangerously sexy, do you know that? What am I asking?" I smacked my forehead with the heel of my palm and guffawed. "Of course you do. That's why you wield your charm like a weapon."

"Let's go inside," he said, taking my hand without waiting for my opinion and towing me toward the door that breached the house from the garage. "Can you hit the button?"

"I sure can," I said, and the garage door lumbered closed as we went into the house.

"I really need a shower after flying. Care to join me?"

"I think I'll sit this one out, or we'll never get out. California's in a drought, remember? Plus, you aren't going to dazzle your way out of this. Honestly, I think I should be pissed at this point that you keep trying to. Do I come off as dumb or naïve, Elijah? Or that unbelievably horny?"

"All right. The shower can wait. If that's what you think I was doing, let's talk first. You can't blame me for wanting to wash the germs from four airports off my body before I touch a single surface in my own home, though, can you?"

"You know what? You're right. I'm sorry. Do what you need to do, and I'm going to go check in with my mom. I've been meaning to call her all week, and the day just gets away from me. If you feel like talking, just come to my room when you're done."

"Hannah . . ." he started, but I was already halfway down the hall.

I felt like a first-rate bitch for saying all that, but I knew when someone was trying to put me off, and that was what was going on. Police didn't show up at our house every day, and when I thought of why I'd been staying here in the first place—because someone had locked me in the walk-in cooler at work—I knew I had every right to know what was going on. The more he tried to shield me from it, the more uneasy I became.

And yes, Hannah Rochelle, you just called this house "our" house.

What was I doing here? I was asking myself in the

emotional sense because this wasn't some complicated, grown-up version of playing house. My heart was getting deeply invested. That meant my heart was also getting dangerously close to being broken if things went badly.

If I were honest with myself, I would admit Elijah Banks had the reputation of a Don Juan. A professional playboy. What made me think I was so special that he would want to settle down with someone like me? I was an inexperienced girl with a ton of baggage.

My mom's mobile number rang through to her voicemail, so I left a quick message and told her I would try to call her tomorrow night around the same time. I needed to log more time ballooning and I wanted to invite my parents, but I wanted to check with Elijah before I did that.

Was it too soon for him to meet my parents? Was that still a thing? Did girls have their boyfriend meet their parents?

Was he my boyfriend?

It wasn't like that was something I could just ask him.

There were times I swore my thoughts of him could summon him out of thin air. Three quiet taps on my doorframe snapped me out of my stressful thoughts about our relationship labels, and I answered the door to my suite.

"Hey, you," I greeted quietly. "Feel better? You smell delicious."

"Thank you, beauty. And yes, I feel so much better. I think that's the worst part about flying commercial. Last time I don't check what Bas has planned for his jet before I have to go somewhere."

"Poor you. So spoiled." I poked his ribs as he walked past me and came deeper into the room.

"You have no idea how much I missed you," he said,

wrapping his arms around my waist and pulling me closer to him.

As much as I wanted him to show me with his talented mouth and sinful body, I needed to ask him who that car belonged to that was in the driveway when I get home from work.

"We need to talk," I said, pulling his arms off me and stepping backward out of the gravitational pull of his heavenly body.

Seeing the look on his face, though, felt like I'd punched him in the stomach, and I felt like I needed to explain myself immediately.

"That sounded so cliché, didn't it? And I'm sorry, it's nothing bad. I mean, I don't think it is? It seems silly now." I waved my hand through the air dismissively and then added, knowing full well I was rambling, "Actually, you'll probably get a chuckle out of it too once I tell you. That's why I haven't mentioned it before this moment."

"Hannah—" he started to say, his tone heavy with warning, so I cut him off.

"Well, that's not true either. I was going to tell you a few times before, but then you would distract me with . . . other things . . ."

Elijah arched one accusing brow, and I felt even more defensive, knowing damn well I was laying blame where it didn't belong.

"For God's sake, woman, just say what you need to say."

"First, promise you're not going to be mad or punish me," I whined, wringing my hands in front of me.

Slowly, he shook his head. "I'm not going to make a promise like that. Not before hearing what you have to say."

Elijah took a step toward me, minimizing the space between us by half then half again with another lengthy stride. "Did you put yourself in danger? Especially knowingly?"

"No. It wasn't like that."

"Okay, tell me what's going on."

"Someone's been calling my cell phone a few times a week. They've mostly been hang-ups, and until whatever that was about with that car today after work, I wouldn't have given it another thought, but now I'm wondering if the two are somehow related."

"Unfortunately, they probably were. Are you okay to sit down with me while we talk? Or do you need to move right now?"

This man.

Tears filled my eyes, and all I could think were those two words.

This man.

"It's okay. We don't have to. You can take laps if you'd feel better."

"No. No, I'd like to feel your arms around me right now. I just don't want you to be upset with me."

"Come." He arranged himself on my bed so he was sitting against the mountain of pillows and headboard, and I crawled into his open arms. He situated us just so and finally spoke again.

"Beautiful, I'm not upset with you. This is my fault. This whole mess is my fault. And I'm so sorry I've brought more drama into your world."

"Can you please tell me what you mean? I don't understand."

"I know you don't. I wish I could ask you to just leave

it alone, but I know that isn't fair, and I know you wouldn't even if it were."

He chuckled at the second part, and I was happy to hear that he really did get me. I could be submissive in some parts of my personality, and in other parts, it would never happen.

"Before you came to stay here a month ago, I'd been casually fucking... I'm sorry, I know that's not what you want to hear, but that's the kind of man I am, or was, or, shit, I don't know—" He scrubbed his hand from his eyes down over his handsome face until it fell like a lead weight onto his chest.

"Elijah, stop beating yourself up, okay? Just tell me what's going on." I knew the kind of man I was getting involved with—or the kind of man he had devolved into over the past few years because of a relationship that had gone bad—but I knew at his core, that wasn't really the man he was. I believed that with my whole heart. But right now wasn't the time for that conversation.

"Grant met her first at a club we all used to go to. It's a pretty safe place for businessmen... umm, like us... to go to because the owner is very discreet. Bas went there before he met Abbigail because everyone signs ironclad NDAs. Anyway, we got sloppy, that's all there is to it."

"Wait," I interrupted. "We?"

"Grant and me."

"I'm not following."

"Uhh... shit. Christ, this sucks. I never thought I'd be explaining any of this to someone, let alone someone I was trying to build a foundation to a future with."

Even though the topic was utter garbage, I couldn't help the ridiculous smile that spread across my lips.

"This is amusing?" he asked incredulously.

"No, I'm not amused, dummy." That made him narrow his eyes, so I pushed his shoulder. "I'm happy. Those words make me happy."

"Help a guy out, here. I'm feeling like the dummy you just accused me of being."

"You said we're building a foundation," I explained, still wearing that silly grin.

He pulled me on top of him so our noses were touching. "You want that too, right?"

Eagerly, I nodded and laughed. I could feel tears pricking the backs of my eyes.

He pressed his lips to mine. It was a gentle, loving kiss at first, but our hunger grew quickly. Elijah bit at my bottom lip to get me to open wider for him and then swept in with his masterful tongue. My head swam with dizzy pleasure that spiked with my pulse and throbbed in all the sensitive places in my body.

When I moaned and squirmed in his embrace, he loosened his hold on me and pulled back to regard me with pupils blown so large, the normally icy green of his iris had all but disappeared.

"We need to finish this conversation. But tonight, beautiful? I'm fucking you."

"Oh." It was all I could come up with in way of a response. Because when Elijah Banks issued that kind of growly comment in your direction, there wasn't much more to say.

We got ourselves under control and picked up the conversation where we'd left it. Elijah begrudgingly explained that he and Grant often shared women, and at one point he shared with Sebastian too, though not as regularly. Apparently, when Grant got serious about Rio, Elijah continued seeing the woman they'd been seeing together by himself.

"Beautiful, I wasn't seeing her. I was screwing her. I don't want you to misunderstand. She wasn't my girlfriend. We didn't go out in public together. Hell, we barely saw each other in an illuminated room."

I held up my hand. "I get it. I don't need gory details."

"Okay. I just want to make sure you do, because she sure as hell didn't."

"Wait. Huh?"

"Well, turns out, she went a little psycho. First Grant left the game of tag we were playing, and then I took my ball and went home too. She didn't like being left on the playground by herself, so she's been acting out like a brat does when they want attention."

"So this stunt today wasn't the first time she tried seeing you since I've been staying here?"

He just shook his head.

I didn't really know how to respond to that. I didn't have the right to be mad. I knew how protective he had been from the start, and I was sure if he thought she were a threat to my safety, he would've done something sooner.

He would've. Right?

"What is it?" he asked.

"Nothing. This is a lot, you know. As strange as it may sound, I like learning about your past, even these parts. Other women. I'm just absorbing it all."

"Honestly?"

"Yes. Honestly. But go on. Let's get to how these dots connect. Or possibly connect. This woman from the playground, as you called it, and maybe my prank phone caller?"

"Well, I'm thinking that may be one of her bratty ways of acting out."

"But how would she have gotten my cell phone number? I'm unlisted. Because of the stuff from my childhood, I've spent a great deal of energy on being safe and untraceable."

"I know people want to believe those things are bulletproof, but they're not. A person with a decent head on their shoulders can find workarounds to the usual systems in place to keep Joe Public safe. And Shawna Miller has more than a decent head on her shoulders."

Well, that just pissed me off because it almost sounded like he had awe for the woman.

"Shawna Miller, huh? Well, if it's all the same, I'm going to give that name to my own private investigator to look into. I don't need some stalker bimbo following me around the city in a jealous bunny boiling fit."

"I don't think that will be necessary."

Christ, was he going to defend her now, too?

"Why's that? Does Rio know about this woman and her fiancé's history? I venture to guess my boss has a mean jealous streak. Maybe we could keep a look out for her together, you know? Like a playground patrol of sorts?"

"Hannah, stop. Your boss has an insane streak a mile wide, so she may just relate to Shawna, not hate her. I just filed a restraining order."

"Wait, you hadn't up to this point?"

"No. There was no reason to. Although, if you had told me you were getting prank phone calls sooner, I may have thought differently about that." His voice had taken a different tone and edginess.

"You said you weren't mad. You're definitely sounding mad."

"Forgive me. I'm frustrated with myself for not seeing this woman's true character before this."

I grimaced. "Well, we often see people resort to desperate measures when they want something they can't have. In this case, you."

My handsome landlord thought for a few beats and then seemed to have an idea. "These phone calls, are any of them on your voicemail?"

I had to jog my memory. "Umm, I don't think so. I can check, though. I have a terrible habit of not deleting voicemails after listening to them. Was she inside the house when you came home?"

He hesitated to answer, which was all the answer I needed.

"How would she have access to all this? Your security system and the guards and a key to get inside at the most basic? Elijah, what the hell? I think there was more to this relationship than you're telling me."

"There wasn't."

"Well, none of this is making sense." I shot to my feet and started pacing. Either he was lying, or he wasn't telling me the whole story. One way or another, details weren't lining up.

"Goddammit." He was on his feet too, then. Wisely, though, he didn't try to contain me. He just raked his fingers back through his hair. Then, as if jolted with a defibrillator, he stopped moving and studied me.

"I'm going outside to call Twombley. I'll be right back."

"Whatever. I'm going to shower. Since you're going outside, I'm locking the door." If he came back to my room, I didn't want him to think I had locked him out. "I hope you're going to fill me in on whatever's going through that mind of yours."

It probably didn't escape his notice that I didn't use any of my usual complimentary words like *sexy* or *capable*.

Honestly, though, at the moment, I wasn't in the mood to be showering the man with my adoration. No, I just wanted to wash away the stink of the day in a hot industrial kitchen and try to clear my head while doing so.

CHAPTER FIFTEEN

ELIJAH

"My brother!"

Grant greeted me with his usual upbeat mood. A day didn't go by when I didn't feel thankful that this man's mental health wasn't completely destroyed by the shitstorm he endured in captivity.

"Hey, big man. I'd ask how you are, but you sound like you just had your dick sucked." I laughed.

"How'd you guess?"

"Oh, Christ. Don't even go there, dude."

"Are you going to try to tell me you and that hot blonde are still sleeping in different rooms?"

"No, not saying that at all." I laughed again. "I just don't want to think about your sex life these days. You know what I mean?"

"We've come a long way, haven't we? Wasn't too long ago we all but shared a sex life." Now he laughed.

"Funny you bring that up. That's kind of why I'm calling."

"Nah, man, I'm pretty sure Rio won't pull a four-way with you guys."

"Ass. That's not what I'm talking about." I rubbed the tension gathering in my forehead.

"Well, it was either that or you want to talk about

Shawna, and I was hoping like hell it wasn't her again. That chick is like a bad penny, isn't she?"

"You have no idea."

"What's going on?" my best friend asked.

So I set about explaining the situation to him. "I got home from the airport this afternoon, and she was inside the house."

"Did you say *in* the house?"

"That's what I said."

"Where was Hannah?"

"On her way home. I got here before her, thank fuck. But according to a disturbing conversation Shawna and I had while we waited for the police to arrive, she thought I was still out of town."

Grant whistled low between his teeth. "Oh, you can't be serious. Dude, she's completely lost it. What are you going to do? Did they take her in?"

"No. I agreed to a restraining order."

"What? Why the fuck didn't you have her crazy stalker ass arrested? Have you lost your mind too?"

"Well, you would be the resident expert, wouldn't you?"

"Don't be a douchebag. I don't want to be called to the morgue to identify you, asshole. I'm sure even your pretty face won't look good dead."

"She's blackmailing me."

"Wait. What?" He choked out both halves of the remark. "Did you just say she's blackmailing you?"

"That's exactly what I said. So do not breathe a word of this to Rio."

"Dude. We don't keep secrets."

"Grant, this could get ugly for you too. That's why I'm calling and didn't bring this to the morning rooftop garden party."

We both laughed at the reference to our new habit of meeting with Bas on the roof of the Shark Enterprises building.

"What the fuck are you talking about, Banks? And you better not be fucking with me right now. We all know I've had enough shit to last a decade, if not more. I just want to have calm, peaceful happiness in my world. Why is that too much to hope for?"

"It's not, my brother. It's not. And I swear to all that is holy, if this little bitch decides to make good on her threat, I will take the fall. Do you understand that? You're right. You've had more than any one person should have to deal with in their whole life—not just a decade. I totally have your back, Grant."

"What's going on?"

Right after he demanded to know the story behind Shawna's blackmail, I heard Rio's voice in the background, and Grant's entire demeanor changed when he spoke to her. Just hearing the difference in his tone sealed the decision for me. I absolutely would fall on the sword for this man. Not just in this instance with this psycho redhead, but anytime he needed me to. From watching him hold his lifeless mother's body in his spindly teenage arms to picking him up in Long Beach a couple months back, I'd seen Grant Twombley suffer for the last time if I could help it.

Just like I'd vowed it regarding Sebastian a year ago when Abbi almost miscarried Kaisan and Grant and I scraped him off the ceiling where he clung with maniacal worry. If I could keep my friends comfortable, happy, safe, and content, I would go to any length to do that.

Maybe it was my way of atoning for the wrongs I'd done. I didn't know. I wasn't a martyr, that was for sure. I lived like a glutton. But the people I cared about didn't have to pay for my sins.

"Banks? You still there? Did I drop you?" Twombley must have repeated himself a few times before he shook me from my introspection.

"Yeah, yeah, I'm still here. You gotta go?"

"Yeah, soon, but tell me the Reader's Digest, man."

I sighed. I didn't want to say it out loud. I knew it was stupid to be superstitious, but we all were anyway. We had been since we were boys running around on the streets. So saying bad shit out loud made it that much truer.

Grant called me on the bullshit, too. "It's not going to make it true or make it happen. Just fucking say it." He chuckled. He knew he was right with the assertion.

"Asshole. There, see? It's true." I laughed too.

"Ha. You're so funny, Mr. Banks. Sense of humor and a monster cock! Oh my God! Will you marry me?"

"I thought you were already taken? Plus, you won't take it up the ass, so what good are you?"

"You could always bottom for me?" Grant teased.

"Never." I got very serious then. "She took pictures of herself after a night of particularly rough play, and she was covered in welts, fingerprints, bruises...you name it. You know how rough that girl could go, man."

"Yeah." He sighed, likely knowing where this was headed.

"She said she will go to the authorities and social media, traditional media, whatever it takes, and say I abused her. Drag you into it too. But like I said," I added quickly, "I won't let that happen. I'll go to fucking prison before I let that happen."

"I'm not worried about that, Elijah. But I understand why you let her get away with the restraining order now. What does she want from you long term?"

"She didn't have a chance to tell me. The cops rolled up and stormed the place. Malibu's finest is a little overzealous when responding to anything, so they actually came into the neighborhood with lights and sirens on."

"Oh, shit, no way."

"Way. It was ridiculous. If Han had been here, she would've been mortified." I laughed just picturing her hiding behind her hands.

"Oh my, shit, brother...was that a little pet name I just heard? Well, hell—"

"Just shut up."

"This is worse...no, wait...better than I thought. I have to go tell Rio."

"Oh, do you mean Blaaaze?"

"Damn straight that's who I mean. You know why I call her that, man?"

"Yeah, duh," I said, pouring it on like a teenager.

But Grant stomped right over my attitude. "Because she's hot as hell. Dude, in all seriousness, we'll get through this mess too. We've been through worse in our lives. Way worse, as a matter of fact."

"I know you're right. I'll see you tomorrow." We ended our conversation, and I took a few minutes to stare out across the sand and just a bit farther to the ocean. The waves were small at the moment, while the tide was calmly in the middle of its never-ending cycle.

Life was so much like the tides. The daily rise and fall of—instead of water level—expectations, excitement, disappointment, joy, sadness, fear, and caution, for example.

Instead of the moon's proximity and, to a lesser extent,

the sun's, we were affected by the people in our daily orbit. Our friends and family exerted themselves to influence our actions and our decisions just like the heavenly bodies pulled the water in the ocean to raise and lower the tide. Whoever pulled the hardest equaled high tide.

Right now, Shawna Miller was my high tide, and I didn't appreciate the way her fucked-up waves were tossing my boat around. Not one bit. It was time to pull this vessel into the marina and get the fuck off. I had to control the things I could and protect the people I cared about. The people I loved. A smart sailor didn't take his boat out to sea in the middle of a spring tide.

With an action plan coming together in my mind, I made a few phone calls while still outside. I could bank on the resistance I'd get the minute I got back inside, so I had to have as much in place as possible beforehand.

The last item on my mental to-do list was to find Marc and give him explicit instructions on resecuring my property while we were gone. I wanted the entire security system scrubbed and reinstated with new passwords and entry codes for everyone.

Back inside the house, I was a man on a mission. I strode toward Hannah's suite with purpose and one intention.

Intention.

We were getting out of this place. Tonight.

"Hannah!" I bellowed her name before I reached her suite, so by the time I reached her door, I didn't have to knock.

She pulled the wide panel open, and I walked her backward until she thumped against the wall of the entryway.

My flat palm covered most of her chest, and she must have been able to read the lust and need in my eyes. I could feel her heartbeat quickly climb beneath the pressure of my touch, and I slid my hand up until my fingers wrapped around her throat.

"Elijah—"

It wasn't just a kiss that cut off her question—it was an oral assault. I could hear the small percentage of my psyche that clung to sanity telling me to slow down, be gentle with her. But then she made this husky, needy, whimpering sound in the back of her throat, and that voice was snuffed out like a candle in an evening breeze.

Finally, I tore my mouth off hers long enough to issue instructions.

"Pack a bag. We're leaving here for a few days. Just the house, not town, so you'll need clothes for work. You have ten minutes to be out in the garage."

One last kiss, with a hard nip to her bottom lip that I know had to sting, but I didn't look back after turning to leave the room again. I needed her to know this wasn't up for argument or even discussion. And smart girl that she was, she didn't utter a single word to my retreating back.

In just under ten minutes, we stood at the back of the black SUV while the security team loaded our bags into the back. The air between us was heavy with anticipation and, from Hannah, something else I couldn't quite put my finger on yet. I'd get to the bottom of it on the drive to the hotel, though.

Carmen had booked a suite for us at the Ritz-Carlton in Marina del Rey through the following weekend. Staying downtown would've been smarter as far as commuting, but I had a need in my blood to be near the water when I slept at night. I suppose it stemmed from my early childhood, but I didn't spend too much time in that cesspool to identify the reason. In the past, when I did see a therapist, most of the appointment time was spent dealing with the abandonment issues left over from Hensley.

"Are you going to tell me what's going on?" Hannah finally asked when we were established on the freeway.

"We're headed to a hotel for a *staycation*." I grinned as I made air quotes around the ridiculous and overused expression.

"Something is so incongruous about you using layman's words like staycation, Elijah Banks." She laughed, catching the playful nature of my comment.

"I made air quotes," I protested. "That has to count for something."

"Nah, it still sounds ridiculous coming out of this mouth," she said as she leaned closer.

Following her physical prompt, I leaned toward her and took her mouth in an aggressive openmouthed kiss. She was glassy-eyed when we finally parted a few minutes later, and her pink lips were a deep rose from extra blood pumping to the surface.

When she went to straighten back to her seat properly, I grabbed her behind the back of her neck and weaved my fingers through her loose braid.

"You know what doesn't sound ridiculous when I say it?"

"I'm truly afraid to ask, when you have that feral look on your face."

My stare just continued to penetrate every single inch of her. Her face, her body. Her mind. Her heart. Her soul. I wanted all of it.

"Okay, I give up. What doesn't sound silly when you say it?" Her voice was my favorite version then. Deeper than the usual alto. Huskier, raspy around the edges, needy and willing.

"That tonight's the night, beautiful. I'm going to fuck you so good, baby, you're not going to be able to walk tomorrow. You're going to beg me to stop and fuck you harder in the same breath. Can you just imagine what that's going to be like, Hannah?" I bit her neck just below her ear, and she moaned so loudly that the security guy, Lorenzo, shot his panicked glance to the rearview mirror to make sure she was okay.

Moving beside her ear again, I said in a commanding but very quiet voice, "Now tell Lorenzo you're fine, because he just looked back here like he's wondering if he has to pull the car over."

She looked at me like I must be joking.

"I'm not joking. Tell him, or no cock for you all week."

After a professional-grade glare, she leaned as far forward as her seat belt would allow and squeezed the driver's arm.

Very kindly, Hannah said, "I'm fine, Lorenzo. Thank you for driving us on such short notice."

"Of course, Ms. Farsey. Of course."

While she was resituating in her seat, the man sneaked a surreptitious wink in the mirror, and I had to bite the inside of my cheek to not smile and get one or both of us in trouble with my beautiful blond chef.

Truth be told, Lorenzo knew what a manwhore I was more than most of the people who worked for me. Because he'd done a lot of driving for me over the past five years, he'd seen a lot of debauchery in the back seats of my vehicles while he got me safely from one point to another.

The man had probably seen my ass more than I'd like to admit. He'd even had the opportunity to get in on the action here and there when the lady I was with just wasn't happy with one dick and insisted on two before I could call

Grant or Bas to come over.

"What was the first thing you learned to cook?" I asked her out of the blue.

"That came out of nowhere." She tilted her head, studying me.

"Yeah, I guess it did." I chuckled.

"Rice Krispy treats."

Now I tilted my head. "Does that count as cooking?"

"Of course it does. You have to measure and mix ingredients, to follow a recipe, I think it totally counts. Even if a person just creates something on the fly, that's still cooking, though."

"Fair enough."

"What about you?" Hannah asked.

"What about me?"

Knowing I also enjoyed cooking, she persisted. "What's the first thing you learned to cook?"

"Hmm. Probably grilled cheese, or maybe tuna casserole."

"What? Are you kidding me right now?" She had her face twisted into a grimace. Even with that she managed to look sexy. Christ, I was hot for this woman.

"No, why? Don't you dare say you don't like tuna casserole. It's as American as apple pie."

"Yeah, but that doesn't mean it's good."

"No, it's not good. It's fucking delicious." I rolled my eyes back in ecstasy. "My grandmother used to make it. We lived with my grandparents when I was a young boy, and she taught me to make it because I loved it so much. She told me the easiest way to learn to cook was to learn to make something you loved to eat."

"She was right. Anytime I've had the chance to teach a

cooking class to kids, that's how I encouraged them to pick what they will make for their final project."

Leaning closer to her, I kissed her nose. "I bet you're an excellent teacher."

"Thank you."

The traffic was typical Southern California gridlock. I hadn't considered the time of day when I hustled us off on this adventure, but Hannah and I passed the time chatting and switching between holding hands, kissing chastely . . . and then not so chastely. I had to rein myself in several times with the reminder that when we got to our hotel, I didn't really want to hurt her, even though the promise had been whispered in her ear on more than one occasion when she sassed off or just when I needed to see her suck in a breath and heave out her tits for me to admire.

Finally, we pulled into the hotel's porte cochere, and Lorenzo helped the bellman unload our bags. I let my security guy know I'd be in touch and reminded him to call if anything seemed amiss in the slightest at the house.

Carmen had called ahead when we were about fifteen minutes away from the hotel, so we were already checked in and immediately shown to our suite by way of a private elevator that the bellhop explained we could access with our room key for the duration of our stay.

I tipped the young man and made it obvious I didn't need a point-by-point tour of the room. I just wanted him to get the hell out as soon as possible. Luckily, the guy was young but not clueless, so he plucked the huge tip I extended toward him from my fingers and was on his way.

Hannah had made mention of freshening up after the long drive, so when I saw the young man out, I made sure the *Do Not Disturb* sign was hanging on the door, locked the door, flipped the deadbolt into place, and turned out any unnecessary lights in the living room. Then I went to find my lover.

The suite had a separate bedroom with a sumptuous king-size bed taking up most of the front half of the room. A sofa and love seat arranged around a coffee table dominated the other half of the bedroom. A massive flat-screen television was mounted on the wall, strategically arranged so it could be viewed both from the bed and the sitting area.

A bottle of champagne was chilling in an ice bucket on a small table in the sitting room, so I brought that into the bedroom and was just working the cork out of the top when Hannah came out of the bathroom.

"Feel better?" I asked, turning to see her all fresh faced and dewy from the shower. The white robe was wrapped snuggly around her, and all I could think about was the fastest way to get between that terry cloth and her skin.

"I do. Sometimes it's so stuffy in a car, even though the air is on and it's perfectly cool." She smiled shyly.

"Can I pour you a glass, beautiful?"

"Oh, yes, please. I love champagne."

"What a coincidence. So do I." I held a flute out for her but made her come closer to me to reach it. With every step she took closer to me, I brought the glass closer to my body until she was right in front of me. I wrapped my arm around her and dragged her flush against me, and together we both took a long drink.

After she swallowed, I covered her lips with mine, this time for a passionate kiss. Her lips tasted of the dry champagne. The perfect combination of grapes and Hannah. I devoured her perfection. I licked my way inside, demanding more when she thought she had given me all she had.

"More. Give me more, Hannah."

She whimpered against my onslaught, and the sound spiked my arousal. Her gasping and pawing at my shirt added to the sum.

"Fuck, beauty, those little sounds you're making are as good as having your hand around my cock."

"Really?" she said while fumbling around my waistband. "I think I'd rather actually have my hand—"

"No. Stop," I commanded, and she stopped immediately. "Get your ass on the bed. Lose the robe."

Aahh, little Miss Brave stared at me with those big blue eyes of hers as wide as she could open them, and yeah, that turned me on too. I was going to need to check myself over and over here tonight because I was at major risk of tearing this girl apart, and she didn't even know it. She didn't even know what I was capable of.

Hannah went to the bed and pulled the covers back, walking the stack down to the foot of the mattress. I swore she was moving as slow as a human could move and still qualify as moving.

"I'm going to count to five, Hannah. If you don't have that robe off and laid neatly across that chair over there and you in the center of this bed, I'm going to spank your ass until it's red. Do you understand me?"

"I understand you," she whispered nervously. But I didn't miss the glitter in her eyes. She was aroused, I was completely sure of it. I couldn't wait to test my theory the second her fine ass was on that bed.

"One..."

For some reason, she stood frozen like a deer in oncoming headlights.

I folded my arms across my chest, barely able to wait to see how this played out.

"Two..."

Something clicked in her brain, and she moved, finishing with the covers on the first side and hustling to the other side.

"Three..."

She yanked the covers down with one hand and was pulling her robe off with the other.

"Four..."

I unbuckled my belt and yanked it from the loops in my pants. The leather made a resounding crack through the air when it doubled back on itself.

Hannah froze mid-action of laying the robe neatly on the chair when she heard the sound, and even I had to admit, it was a dirty trick I'd just pulled. If I really wanted to win this round, I could count her out right here. She'd never be on the bed before I hit five because she stalled to look back when she heard the belt snap.

But she seemed to realize the error of her ways right as the evil grin spread across my lips, and then, in a move that surprised the hell out of me, she took two long strides and dived for the bed like a World Series slugger reaching for home plate. She hit the bed with an *oompf* and rolled to her back, scooting her legs around forty-five degrees to be in the exact position I instructed.

"Five. Holy shit, that was incredible! You are seriously the most amazing woman I've ever met. Do you know that?"

After filling the flute completely, I handed Hannah the champagne glass and undressed while she calmed down from her epic dive across the room. I chuckled a few times, picturing what she'd just done. My dick was so hard it was nearly pointing at the ceiling when I released it from the confines of my boxer briefs. Those damn things were like torture devices once I had an erection.

"I'm going to need another, I think," Hannah said, holding her already empty glass out to me. "No, you'd better give me the bottle if that is going inside me after not having sex for so long."

I climbed onto the bed beside her with the bottle and filled her glass. "This is the last for you, young lady. I never see you drink, and I want you clearheaded for this." I took a big swig straight from the bottle before setting it on the nightstand, then stretched out beside her while she enjoyed her drink— and, apparently, judging by the way she was eye fucking me, the view.

"Do you like what you see, beautiful?" I taunted, reaching down and casually stroking my cock a few times. With a *thud*, I let the steely shaft bounce onto my abs when I released my grip.

Her eyes shot up to mine. "Does that hurt? When you do that?"

Slowly, I shook my head. My grin grew as I watched her process the information and the fact that she couldn't stop sneaking peeks.

"Beauty, look all you want. I love that hungry look on your face. Don't feel like you're doing something wrong."

"Your body is so perfect. I can't stop staring at you."

"That's good, baby. You can look at me while you come for me."

"Elijah . . ."

"Is your cunt wet?"

Those damn impossibly wide eyes studied me, but she didn't answer.

"Answer me, or I'll make you show me. You can stand beside the bed here and touch your toes, and I'll look until I'm satisfied. Pick. Answer me or show me."

For the second time already this evening, she blew my fucking mind when she got off the bed, looked right at me, and then turned her back to me. With one more saucy look over her shoulder, she bent at the waist and gave me a view so stellar my mouth went dry.

"Sweet mother of God." I don't know . . . Was it wrong to think the word God while staring at a woman's cunt? A pussy so pink and dewy and sweet smelling that there wasn't another thing perfect enough to compare it to?

"Stand up."

I waited for her to do as I instructed, and then I asked her, "Do you have a hair tie?"

Most women always had one on their wrist, but because she handled food, my woman didn't always subscribe to the usual trappings of other women. This time, she happened to have what I was looking for, though.

She pulled the band off her wrist and handed it to me over her shoulder. I gathered her hair down her back and quickly braided it in one thick braid. From Bas having Vela in his life, we all were subjected to having a little girl around us at various times. Also, enjoying tying women up and using various equipment for sexual fun and games, it was beneficial to know how to accomplish a braid.

"Now, back down at the waist the way you were. Step apart here." I nudged her ankle with my toes. "About four more inches, beauty. Perfect."

I ran two fingers down her spine from her hairline to her tailbone. Again. A third time.

On the next pass, I used my fingernails to lightly scratch.

"Hannah."

Second pass... "Rochelle."

Third pass... "Farsey."

By that point, she had nice, red welts blooming along her spine, even though I never scratched harder than a light scrape. I took one more swipe while I made the actual point of the entire exercise.

"It's quite possible that you have the sexiest and most beautiful pussy I've ever seen."

And I've seen a lot.

"Thank you," she sighed.

"Turn and rest your forehead on the bed." Together, we pivoted one hundred eighty degrees. "Spread your legs again like they just were. Good girl. You can put your hands on the bed too... or wherever they are most comfortable."

I got down on my knees behind her and, without warning or announcing my intention, buried my face in her cunt. Licking and sucking her folds, I drank down her juices as fast as her body could make them. I could not get my tongue in deep enough. I wanted to become a part of this woman in the worst way.

I used one finger first, tracing her slick and hungry opening, then filling it with my entire finger. When that wasn't enough for her—or me—I added my longer middle finger and reached deeper into her channel. All the while knowing I was readying her for my cock.

Soon I would be balls deep in this same hot, milky spot,

and that thought was making my vision blur at the edges. When I did finally get in there, I'd probably pump twice and burst.

Hannah started moaning into the bedding, and I realized I was so lost in my own desire I hadn't been paying close enough attention to hers.

"That's it, girl. Come for me, baby."

"So close, Elijah. Keep...yes...that...there...yes... God, yes. Please, oh my God!"

I stilled so she could ride out her orgasm on my hand the way she needed and tried to notice what she liked. It was hard to catalog any one thing, though, because she was an unorganized climaxer, as most people were. We'd get better at communicating, though, and eventually I'd be able to get her off in a matter of minutes.

I hooked my arm around her waist, lifted her onto the bed, and climbed on right behind her. When she collapsed onto her stomach, I covered her body with mine and let my erection rest between her ass cheeks.

Her husky moan was utter torture after just watching her come. The fact that my lips still tasted like her sweet, sticky nectar—and that her unique musky smell was so far in my nose I'd probably still smell her tomorrow—coaxed moisture from the tip of my dick. Perfect lubrication to continue sliding between the peach-shaped ass beneath me.

"I can't wait to fuck this ass," I growled. When I pushed up on straight arms, there was enough space between our bodies so I could see my cock thrusting between her cheeks. My comment, however, had her flipping over onto her back so fast, she almost toppled me to the floor.

"Elijah—you're too big for that. It's going to hurt me."

"Not today, baby. Someday, though, and you'll beg me to do it. You'll see."

Before she could say a word of protest, I covered her mouth with mine and stabbed my tongue deep into her. All I could think of was getting inside her pussy.

"I need you to come again."

"I thought you wanted to … to …"

"Fuck you? I do, beautiful. And I will. But I need your cunt nice and pliant so I can get in there. The best way to do that is for you to come a couple of times. That's the way your body was designed."

"You know a lot about these things, do you?"

I arched one eyebrow in a wordless challenge. "Tell me about the first time you remember getting off."

"What?" she croaked.

"Which one of my words didn't you understand?" I sat back on my heels so I could see her gorgeous body laid out in front of me.

Hannah narrowed her blue eyes at me.

"You know that only makes me stiffer, right? That little temper of yours." I ran one hand roughly up the length of her leg and stopped short of her pussy. With my other hand, I gripped myself around the base and squeezed.

Fuck, this feels so damn good.

"The sooner you come again, the sooner I'm going to be inside you. It's what we both want, and you're the one directly in control of how soon it happens."

"But I'm—"

"Do you understand me?"

"I don't remember when—"

"Don't bullshit me, girl. Everyone remembers certain

things in their life. How can you forget coming for the first time?"

"Do you mean with a guy?"

An involuntary growl ripped from deep within my chest at that notion, and Hannah's eyes grew impossibly wider.

"Easy there, big guy." She chuckled but was easily distracted when I tugged on my cock. As if sliding into a different skin, she purred seductively, "Or do you mean do I remember masturbating?"

She was trying to kill me. That was all there was to it. "Yes. Tell me about the first time you touched your little slit until you couldn't stand all those incredible feelings rushing through your body. How old were you?"

One side of her luscious mouth quirked up in a naughty smile. The fire that danced in her denim irises matched the mischief of her grin.

"Naughty, naughty girl. Let's hear it. You're definitely thinking of one story in particular, with all those signs all over your gorgeous face. Tell me the whole thing while I stroke myself. Rub your clit while you do it, because as soon as you come, I'm sliding into you."

"Fuck, Elijah. I want you so bad right now."

"Baby, are you on birth control?"

"No, I'm not. Do you have condoms with you? Oh my God, you brought condoms with you, right?"

"As a matter of fact, I didn't. Will you let me inside your body regardless? I'm clean. I have my latest test results I can show you. I never go bare. But I don't want to have to do that bullshit with you. I'm not joking, Hannah, when I say that this"—I toggled my index finger back and forth between the two of us—"is different."

"I don't know. I mean, we shouldn't take the risk of pregnancy. What would happen if I got pregnant? Elijah, I can't be an unwed mother. My parents would disown me."

"Who says you'd be unwed? I'd put a ring on your finger so fast your head would spin. I have half a mind to do it anyway."

"What?" She stared blankly at me. After a tense few beats, she said, "What did you just say?"

"I said I'd marry you right now. But don't hyperventilate. Shit, breathe, beautiful." I couldn't help but laugh at her reaction to my declaration.

I crawled up over her, pressing her body into the mattress with the weight of my own. I'd been beneath a man before, and I knew how good and how safe and secure a feeling it was. I wrapped my arms beneath her shoulders and held her to me so she could feel my breathing, my heart beating, the very essence of me.

"You are the perfect woman for me. I've seen my share to know, Hannah. I know we haven't been in each other's lives long, but I'm sure you're the one for me. I don't expect you to return the sentiment right now, but I know what my heart wants and what it needs. And it's you."

"Elijah—"

I cut her off with a bone-melting kiss. I poured all the adoration and intense emotion I felt for her into the gesture and hoped like hell she could feel what my body was expressing to her.

"Spread your legs, beautiful," I said with my lips against hers.

It took a few seconds, but slowly, she opened her body to me. And, by doing so, opened her heart to me as well. At the same time, she opened herself to a lifetime of possibility, adoration, and happiness.

"We'll go slow, but I need you to relax, okay?"

Shakily, she nodded.

Inch by inch, I worked my cock into her. When she winced, I stilled and let her adjust. I knew once we got the first time accomplished, it would be easier every time afterward. It would definitely be worth the slow and steady effort with this incredible, expressive creature. When I was about halfway inside her body, I started moving a bit more freely, thrusting in earnest.

"Fuck!" Hannah gasped. "Elijah, holy fuck. I don't... I think... shit..."

Oh, hell yes. Now I recognized these nonsensical babblings for what they were. Her way of announcing the onset of her climax.

"Are you coming, beautiful? I feel you so tight around me. Fuck, baby, so warm and perfect inside this pussy." I buried my face in her neck and pushed in a little deeper.

"Yes, God, yes, I'm coming. Oh—" And then she squeezed her eyes shut and went completely still except for the walls of her cunt showering my shaft with butterfly kisses.

Ecstasy. Pure ecstasy. And one hundred percent mine. That was the final thought that had me coming for the first time inside the woman of my dreams. The last pussy I'd ever come in for the rest of my life.

At least if I had anything to say about it.

We both passed out after that. Hannah—wrung out from stress, orgasms, and the little bit of champagne she drank—tipped over the edge into solid, nightmare-less sleep for once.

I was simply exhausted. Travel always wore me out. No matter what condition I was in physically, how well I ate, and how I managed my stress, I never slept well away from home. With the sexy, snuggly blonde in my arms, I too slept like I hadn't in weeks.

We both had to be into work early the next morning, so when the alarm on Hannah's phone went off, as much as we both grumbled, I pushed her toward the shower. Of course, I gave her body a thorough inspection first, making sure she wasn't too sore. The scratches I had left on her spine last night were long since faded.

My cell phone rang while she was still in the shower, and thinking it a bit early for a phone call, I scooped it up and checked the caller ID. It was Marc, the lead security guard pulling the overnight shift at the house.

"Hey, man," I said, my voice still rough from sleep. "A little early, no? Everything okay? The Mrs. having the baby?" I remembered Hannah telling me that bit of news while talking and hoped that was the reason for the call. Better that than something shitty happening at the house.

He chuckled, and I thought that was a good sign. "No, no. She's still not dilated. So, she's frustrated as hell, but no baby yet."

"Just miss me, then?"

"I'm sorry to bother you so early, and I wish I wasn't calling with shitty information."

"Spit it out, man."

"Ms. Farsey's car has been vandalized."

"What?"

"Yeah, I'm sorry, man."

"What happened to it?"

"Someone spray-painted on it."

"Oh no, you're kidding. Gang shit? Graffiti?"

"No, this looks personal. It says, 'You'll pay, bitch.'"

"Did you pull the tapes? Can you see who it was?"

"No. Last night, when Lorenzo got back from dropping you off at the hotel, we moved her car onto the street. The smaller SUV is having the brakes done today, so we had to shuffle spots in the garage."

"Goddammit."

"Do you want me to call the police?"

"Well, let me talk to Hannah and see if she can get off work. She's going to have to file the report since it's her car."

"All right, I'll wait to hear from you."

I hung up with Marc just as Hannah came out of the bathroom with her phone to her ear. She was listening to someone talking on the other end of the call, and all the color was drained from her face.

In a flash, I was by her side. She looked like she was going to hit the deck if she didn't sit down. She let her arm fall slack by her side, and her phone clattered to the ground.

"Hey, hey. What's going on? Who's on the phone?"

But she didn't reply. She just stared off into the middle distance.

"Hannah!" That made her jump, but at least she snapped out of it.

"They're out," she mumbled and looked at me with giant childlike eyes.

"What? Who? Who's out?" I demanded.

"The Trasks. The couple who tried to kidnap me when I was a child. I had a voicemail from my dad. He got a call from our attorney because I have to be alerted anytime they have a parole hearing." She looked at me, and her eyes were filled with tears. They started spilling over onto her paper-white cheeks.

Plop. Plop. Plop.

Wiping her tears as they fell gave me something to do besides tear apart the hotel room while I waited for her to continue.

"They were granted parole. They both were granted early release." She sat on the edge of the bed and put her face in her hands.

When I tried to comfort her by rubbing her back, she shrugged off my touch. Damn, that stung, but I knew she was panicking, so I tried to not take it personally.

But then it hit me. Her car.

"When did this happen?" I asked, and it came out on a bark.

She shrank bank from my volume, and I felt like a complete jackass, but I was panicking too. How could I not keep her safe? Twice in one day I failed to keep her safe.

"Yesterday morning."

Well, I must not have had the poker face I thought I did, because immediately she said, "What? What is it?"

"Pack your stuff. We're leaving."

"Why? What's going on?"

"I think they've come back to finish the job."

ALSO BY VICTORIA BLUE

Shark's Edge Series:
(with Angel Payne)
Shark's Edge
Shark's Pride
Shark's Rise
Grant's Heat
Grant's Flame
Grant's Blaze

★

Elijah's Whim
Elijah's Want
Elijah's Need

Misadventures:
Misadventures with a Book Boyfriend
Misadventures at City Hall

Secrets of Stone Series:
(with Angel Payne)
No Prince Charming
No More Masquerade
No Perfect Princess
No Magic Moment
No Lucky Number
No Simple Sacrifice
No Broken Bond
No White Knight
No Longer Lost

**For a full list of Victoria's other titles,
visit her at VictoriaBlue.com**

ACKNOWLEDGMENTS

As I step onto the Shark stage as a solo act, I must acknowledge and thank the support team in the wings. The entire gang at Waterhouse Press, who continue to believe in this series and dedicate their time and individual talents to bring you, the loyal readers, this amazing finished product: Scott Saunders, Meredith Wild, Jon McInerney, Robyn Lee, Jennifer Becker, Yvonne Ellis, Kurt Vachon, Jesse Kench, and Amber Maxwell. I'm also thankful for the Waterhouse proofing, copyediting, and formatting teams. Thank you for your keen eye and attention to detail.

My dearest Megan Ashley—Thank you for keeping my professional life organized and running smoothly, and for the friendship, love, and support that has been an unexpected and cherished byproduct of our work engagement. XOXO

To every single member of Victoria's Book Secrets—I can't express how much I love each and every sister in our group. We've grown into a fabulous, caring family. The love and support you show me and one another makes me so proud to call you mine.

Lastly, a special thank you to Amy Bourne for the top-level support and beta reading prowess you provide. I could write an entire chapter on the ways you enrich my life.

ABOUT VICTORIA BLUE

International bestselling author Victoria Blue lives in her own portion of the galaxy known as Southern California. There, she finds the love and life-sustaining power of one amazing sun, two unique and awe-inspiring planets, and four indifferent yet comforting moons. Life is fantastic and challenging and every day brings new adventures to be discovered. She looks forward to seeing what's next!

Visit her at VictoriaBlue.com